Warren the 13th *created by* Will Staehle

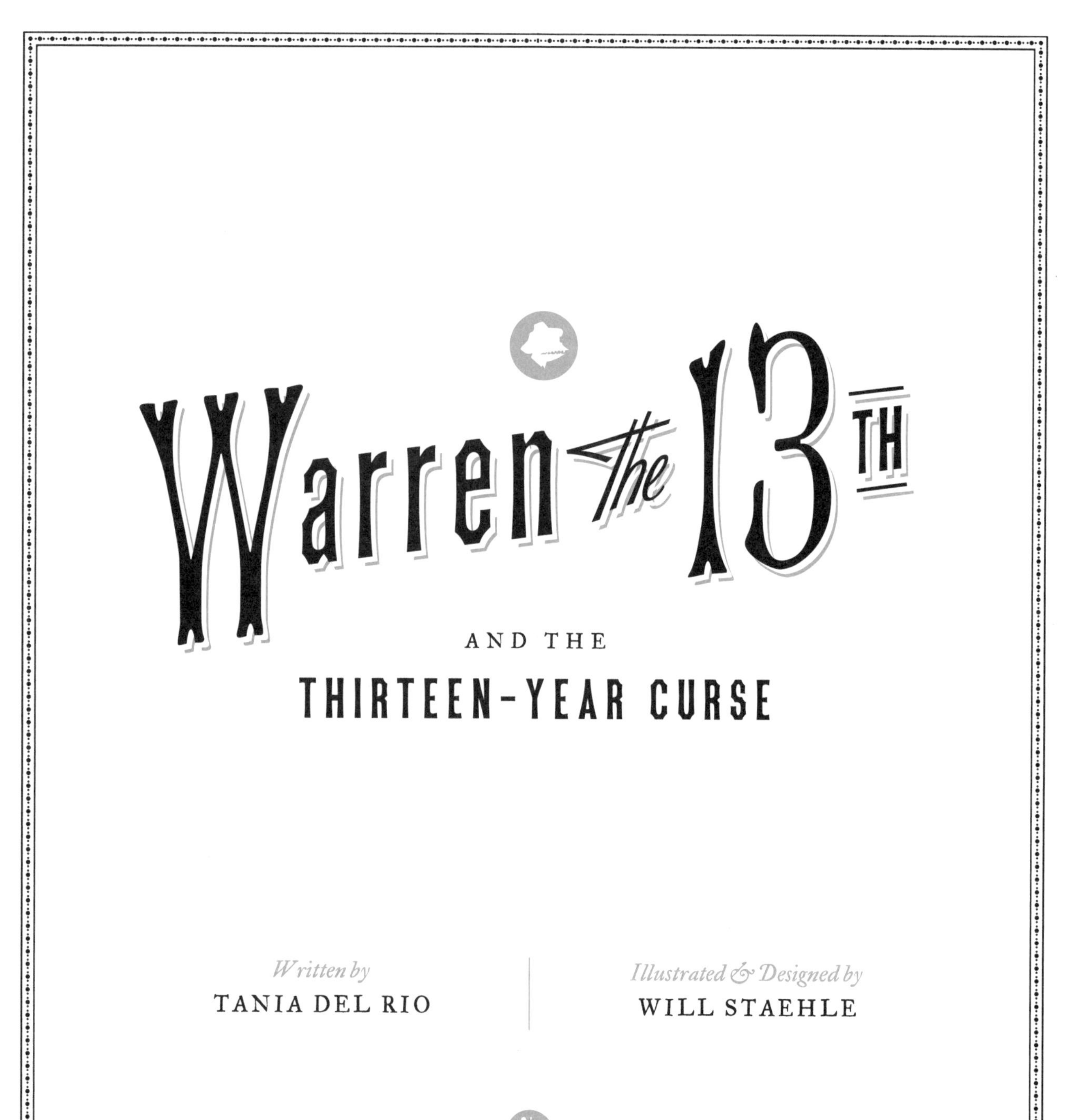

Warren the 13th

AND THE THIRTEEN-YEAR CURSE

Written by
TANIA DEL RIO

Illustrated & Designed by
WILL STAEHLE

QUIRK BOOKS PHILADELPHIA

Library of Congress Cataloging in Publication Data
Del Rio, Tania, author. || Staehle, Will, illustrator.
Warren the 13th and the 13-year curse / written by Tania del Rio ; illustrated and designed by Will Staehle.
Summary: After the Warren Hotel is shipwrecked on a strange island on his thirteenth birthday, Warren and his friends must solve a series of riddles to rescue Sketchy from a travelling circus.
2019037455
CYAC: Hotels, motels, etc.—Fiction. || Orphans—Fiction. || Shipwrecks—Fiction. || Riddles—Fiction. || Adventure and adventurers—Fiction.
PZ7.D3865 Wan 2020 || [Fic]--dc23

ISBN: 978-1-68369-090-0
Printed in China
Typeset in Historical Fell Type Roman
Designed by Will Staehle
Illustrations by Will Staehle
Engravings collected by Unusual Corporation and from Shutterstock.com
Production management by John J. McGurk

Quirk Books
215 Church St.
Philadelphia, PA 19106
quirkbooks.com
10 9 8 7 6 5 4 3 2 1

For:
Camyu and Remy,
Alex and Audrey,
Liam and Violet

TABLE
of
CONTENTS
ENJOY THE RIDE
RIGHT THIS WAY

CHAPTERS

I.

IN WHICH A PARTY IS PLANNED

Dark clouds bubbled on the horizon, bluish black and heavy with rain. Warren the 13th lowered his telescope and licked his finger, holding it up to the air. The wind was blowing southeast, and the Warren Hotel was sailing northward. The storm wouldn't trouble them. Warren sighed in relief. Today was his thirteenth birthday, and he didn't want bad weather to get in the way of the celebrations he'd planned.

He was currently perched in the crow's nest that he'd installed on the roof of his wondrous and world-famous hotel. Not only was the ancient establishment, which his family had owned for generations, able to walk upon tall retractable mechanical legs, but it had recently revealed its ability to transform into a seaworthy vessel as well. Right now, the blue ocean waves were calm, and the hotel bobbed along at a pleasant pace. Warren was eager to know where they'd end up next.

The resident rooftop crows grumbled from the nearby chimney stack, no doubt jealous that Warren was sitting in what should rightfully be their "nest."

Warren sighed. "I told you, this isn't a real crow's nest! It's where crew members scout for land or danger."

The crows were not convinced. They eyed him flintily, their feathers ruffling. Warren climbed out and slid down the wooden pole, landing with a thump on the rickety roof tiles. He always felt like Jacques

Rustyboots when he did that. The legendary pirate was the lead character in his favorite novels; he was also Warren's biggest idol [besides his late father, Warren the 12th, of course].

Warren had always wanted to be like Jacques Rustyboots, exploring the wide-open seas, and now he had gotten his wish. Well, minus the pirating part. Warren didn't want to steal or pillage; he just wanted his guests to be comfortable.

But right now, guests were one thing his hotel was short on. Ever since escaping from the evil Malwoods, the hotel-turned-boat had been drifting across the open waters but hadn't yet hit land, nor had it come across another boat. Warren was eager to arrive someplace he could open the doors and welcome new business. In the meantime, he had other tasks to accomplish—such as preparing for his upcoming birthday party. Now that he was certain the weather would cooperate, he was ready to dispense the invitations.

Glancing up, Warren noticed the cantankerous crows flocking to the vacated lookout basket, where they'd no doubt leave a mess of feathers and droppings. He smiled. The crows were his guests, too, and he was used to cleaning up after them. Suddenly, a shiny object dropped down from the basket; Warren caught it in his hand. It was a battered doubloon, rusted and chipped on the edges.

"A birthday gift, for me?" Warren said, running his fingers over its ridges. One side depicted a bearded king, and the other a grand pirate galleon. This was a real pirate doubloon, just like the one his old importer-exporter friend Captain Grayishwhitishbeard had given him, only this one was much worse for wear.

"Where did you get this?" Warren called up to the crows. The birds cackled mysteriously.

Warren knew the crows had a habit of stealing shiny objects, but how had they managed to get their claws on a pirate coin? Could the hotel be closer to land than he thought?

Warren pocketed the doubloon and opened the hatch that led into his attic room. With practiced skill, he dropped into the tiny space. Since becoming the manager of his family's hotel, Warren could have moved into any of the larger, more opulent rooms. But he loved his humble bedroom, and it had taken him ages to decorate it just the way he liked, with dozens of his sketches pinned across the walls.

Warren reached into a drawer of his bedside table and pulled out the stack of invitations he had been working on earlier that day. They were written on heavy cream paper and fastened with an elegant wax seal bearing the letter "W." It was time to hand them out.

First, he went to the guest observatory on the eighth floor, where Beatrice, the hotel's resident perfumier and protectress, spent most of her time. He could hear the sweet trill of her violin echoing down the hall, which was lined with floor-to-ceiling windows, giving guests a panoramic 360-degree view. The room was filled with an assortment of comfortable chairs and ottomans, as well as a silver cart stocked with hot tea and cucumber sandwiches.

Beatrice was in her usual spot playing a sad tune. Rose tattoos covered every inch of exposed skin, each one representing an evil witch she had captured in one of her magical perfume bottles. Beatrice's voice had been stolen by a witch long ago, so she spoke not a word, instead communicating via picture cards. Warren was getting better at deciphering her messages, but no one was as fluent in pictographs as Beatrice's daughter, Petula.

Beatrice paused as Warren approached, then she reached into her pocket. She produced a card depicting a festive cake and showed it to Warren. He knew this was her way of saying "Happy birthday."

"Thanks, Beatrice!" Warren gave her one of his handmade invitations. "My birthday party is tonight in the ballroom. It's pirate themed. I hope you can make it!"

"Ahem!" sounded a nearby voice.

Warren spun around to see Henry J. Vanderbelly seated in one of the armchairs, writing in a notebook. He was a newspaper reporter for the *Fauntleroy Times* who had found himself stranded aboard the hotel after their escape from the Malwoods. He didn't seem to mind too much, however.

"Oh, Mr. Vanderbelly!" Warren said, scurrying over. "You're invited, too, of course!"

He presented the large man with an invitation, which he accepted with a grin. "Ah, most excellent. I shall look forward to writing an article all about it!"

"Or you could just enjoy the party and not write anything at all," Warren suggested.

"Nonsense! My readers are waiting with bated breath to hear word of my adventures at sea. This is just the sort of content they crave!"

Warren shrugged. Nothing could dissuade Mr. Vanderbelly from his journalistic tendencies.

Next, Warren went down to the fourth floor, which was home to the library that also served as the office of Mr. Friggs, Warren's tutor. As usual, Warren had to scale a mountain of clutter and stacked books just to reach the desk, where Mr. Friggs was frowning over a series of faded maps.

"Oh, hello, my boy," Mr. Friggs said absently. "Is it lunchtime already?"

"We already had lunch, remember?" Warren asked. "An hour ago?"

"Oh! Oh, yes, that we did." Mr. Friggs finally lifted his gaze from the maps and shook his head a little, as if to loosen the cobwebs in his brain.

"Are you O.K., Mr. Friggs?"

Mr. Friggs tugged at the long white mutton chops that framed the sides of his wizened face. He had a habit of doing that whenever he was anxious.

"I don't like this course we're on," Mr. Friggs said, gesturing to his maps. He was the hotel's official navigator and cartographer, responsible for guiding the hotel from point A to point B. Which was a lot easier to do when the hotel was on land and in familiar surroundings.

"But we're not on any course," Warren said. "We're just sort of . . . drifting."

"Ah, that's the problem! We have no idea where we'll end up."

"But that's what makes it fun!"

Mr. Friggs let out a huff. "Fun until we sail into hostile territory or are attacked by pirates! There are a lot of dangers out at sea, and we've now gone beyond the reach of my maps. You know what that means . . . "

"We're in uncharted territory!" they said in unison, though Warren's tone was filled with wonder and Mr. Friggs's was filled with dread.

"And as for today being your thirteenth birthday, well . . . " Mr. Friggs trailed off. "Never mind."

Warren wasn't sure what Mr. Friggs was insinuating, but he was grateful for the change of topic.

"Speaking of which, I'm having a birthday party tonight. In the ballroom," Warren said, handing out his invitation. "I know you don't usually like to leave the library, but—"

Mr. Friggs smiled as he ruffled Warren's golden hair.

Warren gave a little bow and left the library before Mr. Friggs could bring up his worries again.

Now, where was Petula? His friend was usually using her magical portals to teleport all over the hotel as she helped with the daily chores, making it hard to pin her down. Warren decided to head to the basement and the kitchens, where he knew he'd find Chef Bunion and Sketchy, Warren's loyal friend.

As usual, the kitchens were bursting with the clatter of pots and pans and the scent of tasty spices and fresh-baked bread. Chef and his assistant were already hard at work preparing that evening's supper.

"Don't look!" Chef exclaimed as Warren entered. Sketchy let out a shrill whistle. Warren quickly covered his eyes with the invitations.

There was a furious chopping noise to Warren's right, and the sound of eggs cracking to his left, followed by the clang of the oven door. Even with his eyes clamped shut, Warren could envision the familiar scene. Chef would be dicing ingredients with the dexterity and speed he had learned in the circus many years ago, and Sketchy would be using its eight tentacles to perform simultaneous tasks with dizzying skill.

"I have invitations to give you for my birthday party tonight!" Warren said.

"We'll get them later. Now, shoo!" Chef said, not unkindly.

Warren yelped as he felt one of Sketchy's rubbery tentacles wrap around his torso and shove him out the door.

"All right, I'm leaving. You can let go now!" Warren said, and Sketchy dumped him unceremoniously outside the kitchen. The creature pulled the door shut behind it with an admonishing whistle, though not before snatching the invitations out of Warren's hands.

Warren smiled. Well, whatever birthday meal his friends had planned, it smelled delicious.

He had only two invitations left: Petula's and Uncle Rupert's. He knew he'd find his lazy uncle napping in the hammock that he had strung across the hotel's control room. Despite never being trusted to navigate, Uncle Rupert still liked to spend his time near the switches and levers, as though the proximity raised his own importance [at least in his opinion].

Warren passed through the boiler room

and down a narrow corridor. A calming blue light flooded the control room, reflected by the shimmering water that engulfed the cockpit window. This part of the hotel used to be the basement but was now the hull of the ship. It sat below the waterline, providing a unique view of the underwater environs that the rest of the hotel did not have.

Currently, a variety of large colorful fish could be seen swimming past the window, and several little brown fish were nibbling at the algae forming on the edges of the glass pane. Being in the control room was rather like being in one of the wondrous aquariums that Mr. Friggs had once described to him. Warren watched transfixed as a large eel slid by like a sinuous silver ribbon.

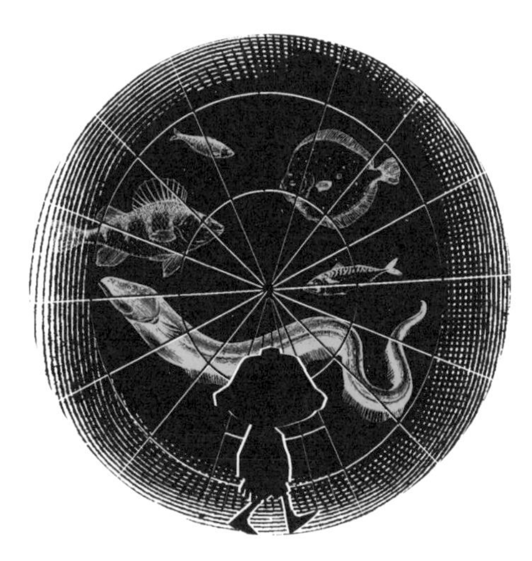

"*HAAARRNNK!*" Uncle Rupert was snoring loudly, disrupting the tranquil mood.

Warren walked over and shook his uncle's sleeve. Lately, Rupert had taken to dressing in what he called "leisure wear": loose-fitting and comfortable clothes, decorated with garish patterns that made his round figure appear even more voluminous.

"Uncle Rupert?"

"HAAARRNNK!"

"UNCLE RUPERT!"

Rupert sputtered awake, nearly tumbling from the hammock.

Uncle Rupert

"What is it, boy? Dinner already?"

"No," Warren said. "I wanted to invite you to my birthday party tonight."

"Birthday party? What do you mean?"

"It's my birthday today!"

"It—it is? Didn't you just have one of those?"

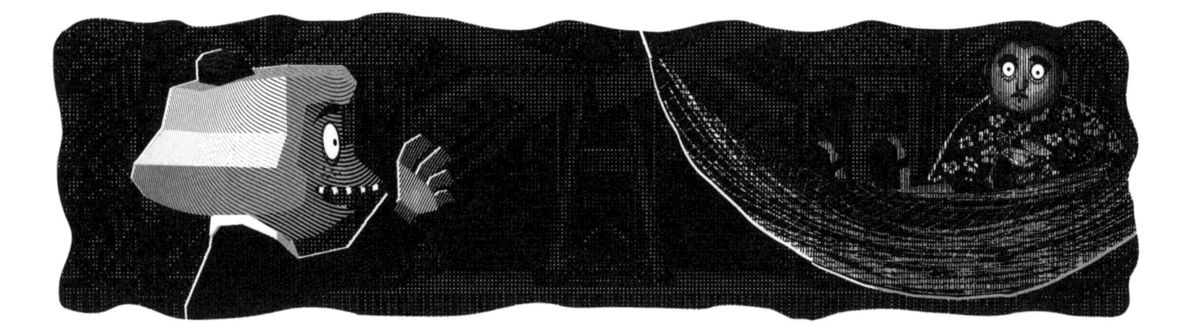

"No," Warren said, trying not to show his hurt feelings. His uncle had forgotten yet again. "I haven't celebrated my birthday since Father died. This is the first year I have friends to celebrate with me!"

He presented the invitation and Rupert read it over, muttering to himself. He then looked up at Warren, eyeing him with suspicion.

"How old are you now?"

"Thirteen," said Warren.

"Th-th-thirteen!" Rupert gasped, and this time he really did fall out of his hammock. He scuttled away like a frightened crab.

"What is it?"

"Unlucky!" Rupert hissed, shielding his eyes. "Cursed!"

"What is?"

"YOU! The number thirteen!"

"Uncle Rupert, you don't really believe in that superstitious stuff, do you?"

"Of course I do! This is your most unlucky year, boy! Bad things will follow you everywhere you go! Just you see! Stay away from me! Better yet, stay away from this hotel!"

"You know I can't do that. I'm the manager!" Warren cried.

"Then we're all doomed. DOOMED!"

"Gee, thanks for the birthday wishes," Warren said glumly. "I guess this means you won't be coming to my party."

There was a long pause.

"Will there be cake?" Rupert asked in a small voice.

"Yes, of course."

"Well, perhaps I'll risk an appearance, then." Rupert sniffed and crawled back into his hammock.

Warren left the control room feeling a good deal gloomier than when he walked in. What nonsense! A person couldn't have an entire unlucky year, could they? Having lost his parents at a young age—not to mention being born with gray skin and a toadlike face and crooked yellow teeth —Warren had often wondered if he was cursed.

But things had gotten so much better ever since he defeated his evil Aunt Annaconda, who wanted to seize the hotel for herself. True, it'd been pretty unlucky when the walking hotel fell over in the Malwoods, but eventually Warren and his friends not only fixed the structure but also defeated Calvina, queen of the witches, and freed the Sapsquatches from her grip. Now Warren was the youngest hotel manager in the world, and he had a new family of friends who made him happy and gave him purpose. He was on a one-of-a-kind ship, exploring the open seas like Jacques Rustyboots. Life was good. Turning thirteen wouldn't change anything. Not really, Warren hoped.

Warren tried to push his anxieties aside as he searched for Petula. He checked the lobby, with its checkered tile floor, wilted potted plants, and flickering chandelier. He checked the game room, with its rarely used snooker table and half-finished jigsaw puzzle spilling across a table. He checked the sewing room—one of Petula's favorite areas—with its elegant sewing machines and coils of colorful thread. He even checked the utility closet, which was cluttered with brooms and buckets and rags. The hotel was just so large, full of corridors and tucked-away chambers—she could be anywhere!

Warren paused his search on the fifth floor, which was home to the Hall of Ancestors. Here hung all the portraits of his forefathers. He realized that he had been so busy all day, he hadn't had a chance yet to tell his father about his birthday plans.

"HELLO, DAD!"

Warren said cheerfully to the portrait of Warren the 12th. His father was a handsome man, painted in bold strokes that matched his strong chin and square shoulders. His father's image, as always, seemed to be looking down, a warm smile on his face.

"As you know, it's my thirteenth birthday today," Warren said. "I'm planning a grand party." A twinge of sadness tugged at Warren as he added, "I wish you could be here to help celebrate."

Warren's father had died when Warren was only seven years old, and since then things had never been the same. Warren hoped his dad would be proud of how he had managed to bring the hotel back from the brink of ruin.

Warren was distracted by the sound of a door closing, and he spotted Petula at the other end of the hall, carrying a large cardboard box.

"Petula!" he called. "I've been looking everywhere for you!" Petula set down the box as he handed her an invitation. "I hope you can make it to my party tonight."

Petula accepted the invitation but let out a sigh.

"What is it?" Warren asked.

"Nothing," Petula said. "It's just . . . must you plan everything?"

"What do you mean?" Warren asked, perplexed. "Why wouldn't I plan my birthday party?"

"Well, didn't you suppose . . . " Petula trailed off. "Never mind. I'm rather busy at the moment, but I'll see you later this evening. Why don't you go take a nap for a few hours?"

Warren was aghast. He had never taken a nap before. Not when there was always so much that needed doing. A nap meant sleeping during the most precious hours of the day—a ridiculous concept!

"But there are decorations I need to hang," he protested. "And I must polish the tables and move the Victrola into the ballroom. Not to mention all the—"

"Yes, a nap!" Petula cut in firmly. "Or at the very least, relax for a while. It is your birthday, after all! You're not supposed to do any work today."

Warren hesitated. She did have a point.

"But what about all the things that need to be done?"

Petula let out a huff and drew a magical portal with one hand. With the other, she grabbed Warren's arm, yanking him into the swirling mist. His stomach turned and his vision clouded with disorienting streaks of light.

Suddenly, he was ejected out the other

side of the portal, landing on the wood of his attic floor. *THUMP!*

"There!" Petula said. "Now, try to relax and don't worry about a thing."

Petula disappeared back into her portal, which closed with a *SHWOOP!*

Warren walked over to his bed, wobbling slightly. Petula's portals always made him feel a little queasy. He flopped onto the mattress and exhaled as he tried to relax. But his mind was still whirring with all the preparations for his party. He checked his pocket watch and saw there were still five hours until the event. Surely a little rest couldn't hurt? In fact, it might be quite rejuvenating.

Warren wasn't feeling sleepy, however, so he reached under his bed, where he kept his stack of Jacques Rustyboots books. He had read them all from cover to cover many times. So many, in fact, that he could recite them from memory.

He cracked open one of his favorites, *Jacques Rustyboots and the Peanut Butter and Jellyfish*, and immersed himself in an unusual story in which the pirate stumbled upon a mysterious island made entirely of food. Just as Rustyboots discovered a buried chest filled with candy coins, Warren drifted off to sleep, dreaming of chocolate turtles and butterscotch rivers.

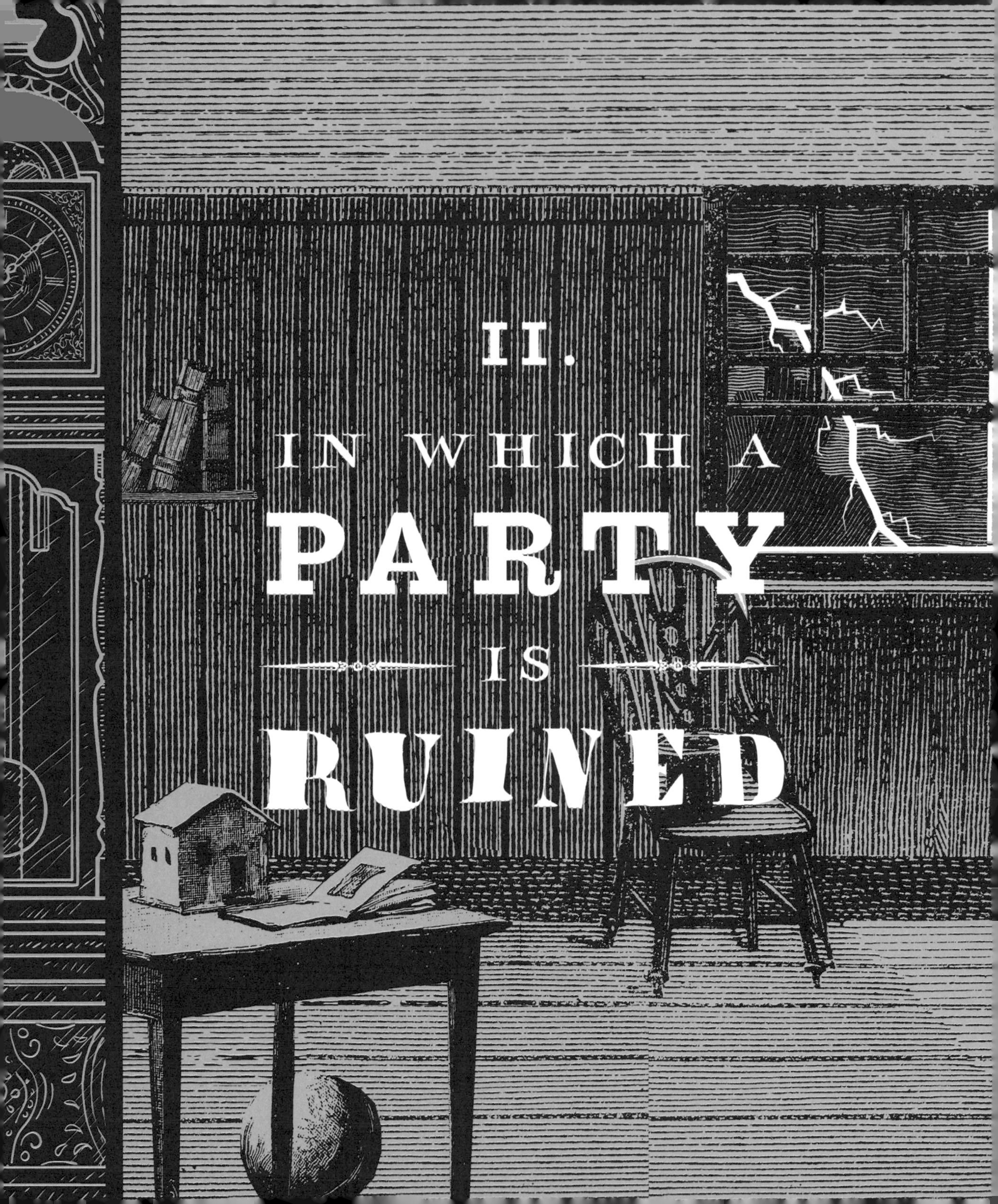

II. In Which a Party Is Ruined

AAAH!" Warren shot up in bed, filled with panic. He fumbled for his pocket watch. He was late! To his own birthday party! He was horrified. "Nothing is done!" he cried as he flew out of the attic and down the stairs. "No decorations! No music! No food!" How could he have overslept? He must have been more tired than he thought, but that was no excuse!

His tiny feet went *PIT-PAT PIT-PAT* as he raced down the stairs, barreling toward the ballroom.

"I'm sorry!" he yelled as he flung open the doors. "I didn't mean to—"

His voice trailed off. The ballroom was empty. A lone candle flickered on the banquet table, barely illuminating the cold, cavernous room.

"Hello?" he called out. The only response was the forlorn sound of his own echo bouncing back.

Had everyone left once they realized he was late? Or perhaps no one had remembered to come in the first place. *Unlucky!* Uncle Rupert's voice resounded in his mind. *Cursed!*

Dejected, Warren slowly walked out of the ballroom and back upstairs. He decided to go to the roof, where he could climb into his crow's nest and feel sorry for himself without anyone around to see him shed a tear. His heart felt heavy as he slowly climbed the ladder leading to the roof hatch and pushed open the door.

"SURPRISE!"

Warren was so shocked, he almost fell off the ladder.

All his friends were on the roof, which was decorated gaily with string lights and balloons. Petula and Sketchy held up a large flag with Warren's profile in silhouette emblazoned upon the fabric. Below it, "XIII" was embroidered in gold thread. The flag snapped smartly in the wind and Sketchy let out a loud whistle as it wiggled its tentacles. The rooftop crows cawed raucously, happy for an excuse to make some noise.

"HAPPY BIRTHDAY!" Chef Bunion said, sweeping Warren into a massive bear hug.

"Oof!" Warren gasped as the air was squeezed out of him. "Are those pudding cookies I smell?"

Chef released his grip and gestured to a large banquet table brimming with all of Warren's favorite foods: mini meat pies with buttery, flaky crusts, cheesy pasta oozing with cream, jellied tarts and fresh fruits in

XIII
F

an array of jewel tones, smoked fish dripping with slabs of honeycomb, a steaming cauldron of zesty beef goulash, and, best of all, a cake constructed entirely of Chef's famous pudding cookies—crispy on the outside, with molten chocolatey goodness in the middle. Uncle Rupert was already helping himself to the feast, smacking his lips loudly as he sampled the various delicacies.

Warren was in awe—but even more so when he spotted Mr. Friggs standing among the others. Mr. Friggs hardly ever left the library! He rushed forward to give his elderly tutor a hug. "Mr. Friggs, I don't think I've ever seen you set foot on the roof before!"

"Anything for my favorite student," Mr. Friggs said, looking a little pale as he wobbled on his cane. "Though I don't much like heights."

Mr. Vanderbelly shoved himself between Warren and Mr. Friggs, his notebook at the ready.

"You should have seen your face!" he said, bellowing with laughter. "Oh, if only I could capture the precise expression in words!" He began scribbling madly in his notebook, no doubt attempting to do just that. "Now, tell me, how does it feel to be the victim of such a shocking surprise?"

"Well, I wouldn't call myself a victim at all," Warren said. "It's actually quite lovely!"

"Lovely! Pah!" Mr. Vanderbelly snorted. "Words like that don't sell papers, my boy. How about 'Marvelous!' or 'Stupendous!'"

"Or 'Mystifying!'" Warren added. "How did this all come together? Especially without me noticing?"

"We're witches, remember?" Petula said, and Beatrice winked as she began playing a slightly-more-cheerful-than-average ditty on her violin.

Sketchy began to dance, whistling happily, and draped the flag around Warren's shoulders with a flourish.

"What's this?" Warren asked, touching the silky fabric.

"Every ship needs a flag!" Petula said. "So we made one for you. Now ships from afar will know the SS *Warren* when they see your banner fly!"

"Thanks, everyone!" Warren said, suddenly overcome with emotion. "For a moment I thought you might have forgotten."

"There's no way we'd forget such an unlucky and cursed year," Rupert said around a mouthful of pudding cookies.

Petula frowned. "Don't listen to him. Thirteen happens to be one of my favorite numb—"

Petula was cut off as the hotel suddenly lurched sharply to the left, a large wave battering the starboard side of the ship. A chilly spray misted the partygoers, who stumbled around trying to regain their balance. The food on the table slid dangerously close to the edge, but then a second wave hit the port side, sending the trays and platters back to their original placement.

Warren said, noticing the black thunderclouds roiling overhead. He had been so distracted by the party, he hadn't even realized the storm had caught up to them. Fat raindrops began pelting the roof and everyone gasped as lightning flashed. An ear-splitting peal of thunder followed soon after, causing the shingles to tremble beneath their feet.

"We're sitting ducks out here! We need to get back inside!" Warren cried as Beatrice briskly opened a large portal.

Another massive wave slammed the hotel, tilting it sharply to the right. The wind was picking up, and the waves were growing more turbulent with each passing second.

"Go, go, go!" Petula said, ushering Mr. Vanderbelly, Chef Bunion, and Mr. Friggs through the opening.

"What about the food?" Rupert wailed, clinging to the banquet table's legs as the entire thing slid across the roof toward the starboard side.

"Uncle Rupert! Let go!" Warren cried, lunging forward.

He grabbed onto the man's ankles with one hand while clutching his flag with the other. Rupert's heft was too much for him, and they both began to slide across the slick tiles toward the edge of the roof. At the last second, Sketchy's tentacles reached out and saved them from certain doom.

The table, however, with all its delicious dishes, did not fare so well. Warren watched in horror as it toppled over into the raging sea below. Tarts and pies and pudding cookies rained down with a *SPLISH SPLAT SPLASH* and were quickly devoured by frothing seafoam.

"NooOOoOoooo!" Rupert cried, as though his best friend had just been lost overboard instead of a grandiose meal.

"Never mind that!" Warren cried, even though his own heart was breaking at the sight of all that delicious food gone to waste. "Get into the portal!"

With Sketchy's help, he shoved his plump uncle into the portal, urging Sketchy to quickly follow. Beatrice gestured for Warren to go next, but the boy shook his head. A good manager always put his guests' safety before his own.

"Petula next!" Warren yelled, but his voice was drowned out by the howling wind. The rain was falling in icy sheets, and lightning crashed around them. *BOOM! BOOM! BOOM!* Warren's golden curls were flattened against his skull, drenched with a mixture of rain and ocean spray.

Petula's eyes widened as she pointed to something behind him. Warren spun about and blinked. It appeared to be a strange dent pressed into the ocean, as though by an invisible finger; Warren stared at it, transfixed. The dent deepened and widened and that's when Warren realized what was happening—an enormous whirlpool was forming!

The churning water flowed clockwise, faster, and faster, and faster. The hotel's frame shuddered as it was caught in the edges of the vortex, and the building began to spin like a top. If Warren didn't act quickly, the entire hotel would be swallowed by the whirlpool's gaping mouth!

He felt Beatrice's hand close around his arm as she pushed both him and Petula into her portal. They landed with a thump on the other side, on the control room floor, where the party guests stood in a daze, dripping puddles onto the floor. From deep within the belly of the hotel, Warren could no longer hear the thunder crashing outside, but he could feel the force of the water pressing in from all sides, the wooden walls creaking and groaning in protest.

The portal closed with a loud *SHWOOP!*

"What about Beatrice?" Warren cried.

"She's going to use magic to try to stop the hotel from getting pulled in!" Petula cried. "But you need to help!"

Warren dashed to the controls and grabbed the wheel that steered the hotel. It was spinning wildly and it took all of Warren's strength to grab the prongs and pull it to a stop. "Nnngh!" he groaned as he struggled to turn the wheel in the opposite direction. Chef Bunion ran forward to assist, and with the help of his burly arms, they managed to turn the wheel and halt the hotel's mad spinning. But it still wasn't enough to pull them out of the swirling waters.

Warren yanked on the periscope and peered through the viewfinder to see how Beatrice was doing on the roof. She was a powerful witch, but he still worried for her safety.

He could see her uncoiling the rigging on the mast. With a wave of her hands, the rope seemed to come alive. Wiggling and writhing like a snake, it shot out from her hands and out of sight.

"What's she doing?" Warren cried. He had never seen this type of magic before.

Petula nudged him aside and peered through the periscope.

"She's doing rope magic!" she said, looking concerned. "Sometimes we use it to lasso evil witches who are trying to escape . . . but she's trying to use it on the hotel!"

"That's how she'll pull us out of the

whirlpool!" Warren said. "Great idea!"

"I just don't know if it will work on something as big as the hotel," Petula said. "It's a tricky sort of magic. Ropes don't like to behave."

Warren's attention was pulled back to the control room as water began to spray through the edges of the glass, and the lights flickered and buzzed. Sketchy used its tentacles to try to plug each hole that formed, but there were just too many sprouting up between the cracks. The view beyond the window was a blur of blue and white streaks as the whirlpool raged around them.

"There's too much pressure!" Warren cried. "The hotel is going to be crushed!"

The steering wheel began to vibrate and shake as the connecting machinery was battered by the force of the water. There was a loud *SNAP!* and Warren glimpsed a large wood panel tumbling past the window, where it quickly vanished into froth. "The rudder's gone!" Warren yelled. "We can't steer!"

"CURSED! DOOOOOMED!" Rupert's voice wailed above the sound of splintering wood.

There was a loud *CRACK!* and the hotel residents screamed as the control room went black.

III.
IN WHICH
THE WARREN
IS SHIPWRECKED

orning broke, creating slats of sunlight filtering in through the cracks and holes that marred the hotel's facade. The storm had long since died down, and gentle waves lapped against the sides of the building, which lay lopsided on a sandy beach.

Shipwrecked, Warren thought with a sinking feeling as he stood outside the hotel, surveying the damage. Shipwrecks were an essential part of the Jacques Rustyboots stories, and they were usually followed by thrilling adventures. But this was no story. It was real life, and until the rudder was replaced and the holes patched up, his hotel wasn't going anywhere. On the plus side, however, they had landed on a mysterious uncharted island, and that was rather exciting, indeed.

It appeared to be a small island, densely covered with tropical trees and foliage in varying shades of green, punctuated by bright pink, purple, and orange bursts from a variety of flowers and fruits. A pleasant scent wafted on the breeze as wild birds and monkeys shrieked loudly inside the jungle.

"In any other circumstances, this would make for a lovely vacation spot," Petula mused.

"Well, this may end up turning into a long stay," Warren replied, "unless we can find some supplies to fix the hotel with. How is your mother doing?"

"She's resting," Petula said. "I think she'll need a few days to recover, at least."

Beatrice's magic-rope trick had been successful and Warren was grateful. Unfortunately, her efforts had cost her dearly. Her magic was more suited to catching evil witches than fighting acts of nature, and she was found barely conscious after the whole ordeal.

As for everyone else, thankfully they had emerged from the experience unscathed. Mr. Friggs was back in the comfort of his library, and Mr. Vanderbelly was perched on the hotel's crooked front steps, scribbling an article in his notebook about the "Disastrous Near Destruction of the Warren Hotel" and muttering to himself in dramatic tones. Chef Bunion was nearby, collecting tropical fruits from a tree, no doubt eager to incorporate them into his recipes, and Sketchy was splashing happily in the waves. As for Uncle Rupert, he was napping on the sand and developing a rather unfortunate sunburn.

"I better go scout the island and see if there's anyone who might be able to help," Warren said.

"You're not going alone," Petula said firmly. "Besides, you'll need my portal to return to the hotel in case we run into danger."

Warren nodded. She made a good point. "Chef!" Warren called. "Petula and I are going to look for help."

"Aye, aye, Cap'n!" Chef said as he shook a tree, knocking more fruit from its branches. "Be careful out there!"

Sketchy whistled sharply and wiggled its way up to Petula and Warren as they began to head toward the jungle. It shook its body like a dog, sending seawater and sand flying in all directions.

"Sketchy, I'm sorry, but you can't come with us," Warren said. "You can't fit through Petula's portal, and we need an escape route in case anything happens."

Sketchy lowered its bulbous head and let out a sad trill.

"You have a more important job to do," Petula said, patting it on the back. "You need to guard the hotel until we return."

"What do you say, Sketchy?" Warren asked. "Can you stay here and keep an eye—er , eyes—on things?"

Sketchy nodded and let out a short whistle, although it still watched forlornly as the pair walked off. Warren felt bad leaving his friend behind, but it was for the best.

No sooner had he and Petula entered the jungle than the temperature seemed to rise by several degrees and the air moistened with humidity. Warren fussed with his golden curls, which were getting frizzier by the second. He knew it was vain, but his hair was the one part of his appearance that made him proud. Unfortunately, this climate was not conducive to a handsome coiffure!

All around them were the sounds of chattering birds and critters, but it was nearly impossible to actually see anything, so camouflaged were they amidst the dense vegetation. Warren's and Petula's feet squelched over the rotting undergrowth that blanketed the jungle floor as they navigated around protruding vines and roots. They walked mostly in silence, keeping their eyes and ears open for danger, but also appreciating the symphony of sounds as well as the perfumed air.

Suddenly, Warren heard a distinct rustling coming from behind them and froze. Petula paused, too, and looked at him questioningly.

"I thought I heard something following us," Warren whispered. "But it may have been my imagination."

They stood as still as statues, waiting and watching. But they heard no sound, other than the noisy animals still chattering and chirping in the trees above.

After a few moments, they continued walking, slightly warier than before. But Warren did not hear the sound again.

"Maybe we ought to turn back," Petula said after a while. "My portal may not be able to reach the hotel from here."

Over the past few months, Petula had been practicing her magical abilities and managed to increase the distance her portals could reach from one hundred feet to almost a mile, but the farther the distance, the riskier it was.

Warren stopped and squinted. He saw something—a slash of white through the tangled web of branches ahead. "Wait. What's that?"

They crept forward, cautiously, and used their hands to part the thick waxy leaves blocking their path.

It was . . . a building. But not the type of building that Warren ever would have expected to see in a place like this. It was a pristine and modern structure, with smooth white walls and turquoise trim and a red stucco roof. The area around it was clear of vines and unruly vegetation, with the building sitting on a perfectly manicured lawn. Situated nearby were a patio table and chairs, complete with brightly pattered cushions and a colorful beach umbrella. Petula pointed toward a large sign that stood near the building's entrance, but it was angled and Warren couldn't quite make out what it said. In any case, it all looked perfectly welcoming and safe, and Warren and Petula relaxed.

"I guess we better go check it out!" Warren said cheerfully. "With a nice building like that, whoever lives there is bound to have some supplies that could help us."

They straightened from their crouched position and walked across the soft grass toward the building.

Suddenly, they heard a loud *WHOOSH!* and Warren and Petula cried out as a large woven net fell over them. In an instant, they were swooped up into the trees, where they dangled helplessly, all jumbled together.

"A trap!" Warren cried, trying to adjust his body so that Petula's elbow wasn't digging into his side.

"Hey, watch it!" Petula grunted, pushing Warren's heel out of her face.

"Ahoy, there!" a gravelly voice shouted from below. "What scoundrels dare trespass upon our turf?"

Through the lattice of the netting, Warren could see several burly and grizzled pirates standing below. The men had tough,

wrinkled, leathery skin and white beards. The women had frizzy gray hair and sinewy, well-muscled arms. Though they were elderly, they looked strong. And angry. One of them snarled at Warren and Petula, revealing a mouth with no teeth, only pale gums.

"We mean no harm!" Warren cried back. "We've been shipwrecked upon your shores and were simply looking for help!"

One of the pirates spat. "A likely story! Hah! You were clearly sent here to scout our hiding spot and bring your crew to take it over! Well, we may be old, but we weren't born yesterday!"

Petula frowned. "That's exactly what it means to be old."

The pirates exchanged confused looks.

"No lip from you, young lady!" snapped the lead pirate. His beard was plaited into a thick white braid, and tufts of hair poked out from his ears. His head, however, was as bald as an egg and gleamed in the sunlight. His most frightening feature was his teeth. They were filed into sharp little points, making him look like a shark.

"Arr, what should we do with them?" one of the other pirates asked. He wore a tattered bandana and a leather jerkin. His skin was covered in faded tattoos depicting anchors and other nautical subjects.

"I say we feed 'em to the jungle wolves," one of the lady pirates hissed.

"The jungle wolves!" Warren cried in horror. He had read all about the terrible jungle wolves in a Jacques Rustyboots novel, *Jacques Rustyboots and the Shiver Me Timber Wolves.*

"Let us down!" Warren said in his most managerial tone. "We'll leave you alone if that's what you want!"

"Arr, I don't think so," the bald, sharp-toothed pirate said with a menacing grin. "You be in our territory now, which means you belong to us!"

Warren swallowed nervously.

the pirate said to his companions. "I'll check the surroundings, make sure they be alone!"

"Aye, aye, Sharky!" the other pirates said, and began pulling on a rope to lower Warren and Petula to the ground.

"You mean, that guy's not the boss?" Warren whispered to Petula. This "Sharky" was so scary looking, Warren dreaded finding out what the actual boss looked like.

"As soon as they let us out of this bag, I'll be able to draw a portal," Petula whispered. "It may not reach all the way to the hotel, but I can get us as far away as possible. Be ready!"

But the pirates did not seem to have any intention of letting Warren and Petula out of the netted bag. Instead, they dragged the two like a sack of potatoes toward the building.

"Ow! Ow! Ow!" Warren and Petula yelped as they tumbled about, kicking and poking each other accidentally.

Once inside the building, they were relieved to be dragged over a more forgiving surface, for the interior had smooth tiled floors. The pirates pulled them through a lobby into a large room filled with comfortable easy chairs that were occupied by a number of elderly pirates.

Warren's captors dumped the bag containing him and Petula in the middle of the floor and Warren was surprised to see many of the pirates pause from reading newspapers, knitting, or sipping cups of tea as they turned to watch the commotion. They seemed nothing at all like the mayhem-loving scoundrels he had read about in his Jacques Rustyboots books. What was this place?

"Where's the boss?" demanded one of their captors.

"I'm right here!" a young voice replied.

To Warren and Petula's astonishment, a girl, who looked even younger than they were, strode into the room. She had tanned skin and a cloud of curly black hair, and she was dressed like a true pirate, with a fancy buttoned coat and shiny black boots. A bright-red parrot perched on her shoulder, eying them suspiciously.

"What have we here?" she demanded.

"Filfy treshpashers!" the toothless pirate said. "Spiesh!"

"We're not spies, and we didn't mean to trespass!" Warren said. "We were shipwrecked on the beach and are simply looking for help!"

"How'd you know where to find us?" the girl asked, her dark eyes narrowing. "We like to stay off the beaten path."

"It was pure chance!" Petula said. "We've been wandering the jungle for hours and were about to turn back when we stumbled upon your . . . place. Whatever it is."

"This place," the girl said haughtily, "is called Calm Waves Retirement Home for the Formerly Sea-Faring and Adventurous. Or CWRHFSFA for short." Warren thought it was a rather difficult acronym, but he kept his opinion to himself.

"CWRHFSFA!" squawked the parrot.

"I'm the manager, Bonny. And I happen to be the youngest manager in the world," she said proudly.

"My name is Warren the 13th and I'm a manager, too!" Warren said. "Of a traveling hotel."

Bonny frowned. "How old are you?"

"I just turned thirteen."

"Ha! I'm ten. I'm still the youngest!"

"That's great," Warren said. "We young managers should stick together! Now can you please set us free?"

"Not until you tell me why you're really here. You're not trying to take over my business, are you?"

"No!" Warren said. "I told you: we're shipwrecked. We need to fix our hotel so we can leave."

"Arrgh, what be this?" came a familiar voice. Warren gasped as an old friend walked into the room, his peg leg clacking on the tile.

"Captain Grayishwhitishbeard!" he cried.

"You know each other?" asked Bonny.

"Yes! He was once a guest at my hotel!"

"Yarr, set these two free," Captain Grayishwhitishbeard said. "They mean no harm."

"Hmph. You're not the boss here, even if your first name is Captain."

Captain Grayishwhitishbeard unhooked the cutlass from his belt and held it aloft. "If you won't set them free, I will!"

"You dare go against me?" Bonny said, unhooking her own cutlass. It seemed a sword fight was about to occur, and Warren couldn't help but feel a rush of excitement. Finally! Pirates acting like, well, pirates!

But suddenly, Sharky burst into the room. "Bonny! They've been followed!" Oddly, as he announced this news, Sharky didn't look upset at all. In fact, he looked almost delirious with joy.

"Ha! I knew they were lying!" Bonny said, instantly forgetting her feud with Captain Grayishwhitishbeard. She pointed her cutlass toward the entrance.

"Bring the trespassers in here at once!"

Sharky stepped aside and flung open the doors. With a loud whistle, Sketchy entered, waving its tentacles threateningly.

"Sketchy!" Warren cried.

What happened next, Warren could hardly believe. All the elderly pirates in the room let out a collective gasp and dropped to their knees, their old joints popping and snapping. Then they began bowing and chanting as though Sketchy were royalty.

Sketchy blew a confused whistle and lowered its tentacles. Its many eyes blinked as it took in the scene.

Warren was confused, too. He instantly recognized the term from his books. A common theme throughout the series was Jacques Rustyboots searching for a mythical sea deity called the Great Eight.

"Oh, Great Eight, we welcome you!" the bald pirate blubbered, prostrating himself before Sketchy. "You grace us with your presence!"

The only person who seemed unaffected by Sketchy's appearance was Captain Grayishwhitishbeard. He was using the current distraction as an opportunity to cut the ropes encircling Warren and Petula. Bonny didn't even notice; she, too, was staring at Sketchy with her jaw hanging in shock.

"What is going on?" Petula murmured.

"That's what I'd like to know!" Warren replied.

"It is real," Bonny whispered in awe.

IV.

IN WHICH SKETCHY IS WORSHIPPED

he pirates joined together to hoist Sketchy into the air and parade it around the room. Sketchy let out a pleased whistle. It seemed to enjoy the attention. Bonny's eyes were as wide as saucers and she was whispering something into her parrot's ear. She seemed to momentarily forget that Warren and Petula were there and didn't even seem to care that they had been freed from the net, thanks to Captain Grayishwhitishbeard.

"GREAT EIGHT! GREAT EIGHT!" Bonny's parrot cheered, flapping its wings.

"Why are they calling Sketchy the Great Eight?" Warren asked, turning toward Captain Grayishwhitishbeard, who appeared almost bored by the strange scene.

"And why aren't you acting like the other pirates?" Petula added.

"Because I'm no pirate!" he said, huffing.

"Oh, right. You're an importer exporter," Warren said.

"But mostly importer," Captain Grayishwhitishbeard reminded him.

"Very well," Petula said. "Why are the pirates acting that way about Sketchy?"

"Arr, I'll explain on the way back to yer hotel," Captain said. "It needs some fixing, right? These pirates may be old, but they're the best at making a vessel seaworthy. It's in their blood!"

He raised his voice and waved his cutlass in the air. "Yarr, if ye want to please yer Great Eight, come and repair its boat! This group's been shipwrecked, and they need a hand or two!"

The pirates cheered, eager to help.

"Wait a minute!" Bonny cried, snapping out of her trance. "You can't just leave! There are release forms . . . and liability clauses!"

But the pirates ignored her. With Sketchy firmly resting upon their shoulders, they marched out the door, chanting and cheering. Some pirates hobbled ahead to scatter tropical flower petals on the ground, carpeting Sketchy's path.

"Make way! Make way for the Great Eight!"

"Come back! That's an order!" Bonny yelled, but not a single pirate took heed, not even the cronies who had captured Warren and Petula.

"You can come with us, if you want, Warren suggested to Bonny. "We could always use another hand, and we'll make sure everyone returns here once the job is done."

"I'm not leaving, and neither are you!" Bonny said, brandishing her cutlass and stepping in front to block their exit. "You're my prisoners, remember? I forbid you!"

"*You heard her!*" screeched the parrot.

"Sorry," Petula said, and with a flick of her wrist, she drew a portal and yanked both Warren and Captain Grayishwhitishbeard through it.

They emerged in the jungle, several yards ahead of the procession carrying Sketchy.

"Yarr, that was topsy-turvy!" Captain Grayishwhitishbeard said, clutching his stomach.

"You never quite get used to it," Warren agreed.

"Stop complaining. I got us out of there, didn't I?" Petula said. "Oh, what an annoying girl that Bonny was! She's not very bonny at all, if you ask me."

"It's tough being a young manager," Warren said. "I feel a little sorry for her."

"After the way she treated us?" Petula scoffed.

"Arr, she's not too bad . . . usually," Captain Grayishwhitishbeard said. "She runs a tight ship at yar retirement home, but she cares, she truly does."

"Speaking of which, how did you end up in a place like that?" Warren asked.

"Mutiny!" Captain said, sighing bitterly. "Months ago, me crew rallied against me and gave me the boot. Said I was too old to be an importer exporter. They dumped me on this here island to live out me days."

"That's terrible!" Warren said. "Especially since you don't look old at all."

It was true. Despite his name, Captain Grayishwhitishbead had a lustrous and thick black beard, though Warren knew his secret: hair dye. Even so, he seemed more robust and energetic than the elderly pirates wobbling and gasping under Sketchy's weight.

"Hey, you can put Sketchy down!" Warren yelled to them. "It's perfectly capable of walking on its own."

Sketchy belted out an offended whistle.

"Now, don't let all this attention get to your head," Warren scolded as Sketchy was lowered to the ground. "I'm still upset that you followed us when I told you to stay put."

Sketchy replied with what sounded like a haughty whistle, but it began to slither on its own. The pirates surrounded it adoringly, still scattering flower petals.

"You never explained why the pirates are worshiping Sketchy," Petula said. "It's so very odd!"

"Arr, pirates believe in a sea deity called the Great Eight," Captain Grayishwhitishbeard explained. "They pray to it for calm seas and luck finding booty. Some say it guards over the biggest treasure hoard in the world. It seems they think your tentacled friend is the Great Eight itself!"

"I always thought the Great Eight looked like a giant whale with eight fins," Warren said. "At least that's how I imagined it while reading my Jacques Rustyboots books."

"Bah! Rustyboots!" Captain Grayishwhitishbeard spat. "The worst importer exporter I ever met. And my most hated rival!"

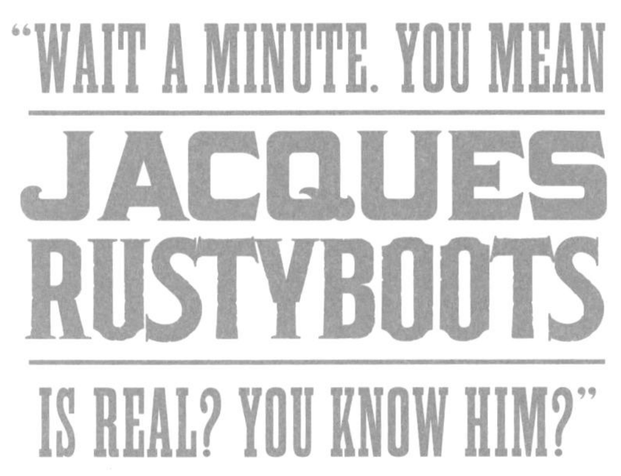

"Knew him," the Captain grumbled. "And what a relief it was when he disappeared all those years ago. Some say he was lost at sea searching for the Great Eight. 'Twas all he ever cared about, the old fool."

"I don't believe it!" Warren cried. "He's—he's my hero! I've read all his books. He's the greatest pirate who ever lived!"

Captain Grayishwhitishbeard snorted. "He's no hero, he's a scoundrel. Yarr, and with a huge ego, at that! Half o' his stories are lies."

"What did he ever do to make you dislike him so much?" Petula asked.

"He swiped all my imports before I had a chance to export them! That and he never shut up about the Great Eight. It was the Great Eight this, and the Great Eight that. He was obsessed with the number eight. Mighty tiresome, if you ask me!"

"So, does this mean Sketchy really is the Great Eight?" Warren asked, looking back at his friend. It was hard to believe that such a funny-looking creature could be so venerated within the pirate community. At the moment, Sketchy was chirping and preening under all the attention.

"Harr! Not at all!" Captain laughed. "First of all, yer friend isn't all that big, is it? Though I dare say it resembles what the Great Eight is said to be. But that's a legend, matey. No truth to it at all. Pirates are a hopelessly superstitious lot. They'll believe just about anything."

As if on cue, the men began to sing in unison. Warren listened to the lyrics as Sketchy whistled along, clapping its tentacles to the beat.

Oh, the Great Eight is the ruler of the seas
It hides in the mist and does as it please!
No ship can ever truly draw near
For the Great Eight it will swallow, and it disappear!
But if a pirate is worthy, only then will they find
The Great Eight's lair and its hidden gold mine!
Many have searched, but all have since perished
The Great Eight awaits only one it can cherish!
With eight legs it will bestow eight shining treasures
To all the rest, it will destroy with displeasure!

"That doesn't sound like Sketchy at all," Warren said, slightly relieved. If his beloved pet really was an all-powerful sea deity, he was pretty sure he would have figured it out by now.

Before long, the motley group reached the hotel. The pirates needed no instruction: they instantly set to work like industrious ants, hammering loose planks into place, patching holes, and replacing the broken rudder with a jungle tree wood that was stronger and more flexible than the original. True to Captain Grayishwhitishbeard's word, they did an expert job of repairing the hotel, and Warren was touched by their charity.

⚓ ⚓ ⚓

By the time the repairs were finished, night had fallen and it was too late to set sail, so Warren made an announcement.

"In thanks for your hard work making the Warren Hotel seaworthy again, I invite you to spend the night as my honored guests! There are plenty of rooms for everyone, and I hope you'll find them comfortable!"

The pirates cheered loudly, and Warren's heart burst with pride. Even if it was only for a night, nothing made him happier than extending hospitality to others.

"I say that calls for a celebratory feast!" Chef Bunion said. "Fortunately, I have just the thing prepared!"

With Mr. Vanderbelly's help, a banquet table laden with food was brought out and set up on the beach. Petula used her magic to light torches all around, giving the surroundings a warm and festive glow. The pirates cheered again as they gathered around, eager to eat. Tears of joy streamed down Uncle Rupert's sunburned face, even though he had barely lifted a finger to help with the repairs.

The meal was especially delicious, thanks to the unusual foods that Chef had discovered on the island, and the pirates ate hungrily and noisily.

"Arr, this be much better than the slop served at the retirement home!" Captain Grayishwhitishbeard said, biting into a spiced meat roll wrapped with charred tropical vegetables.

"Chef Bunion is the best!" Warren agreed, nibbling on a skewer of grilled island fruit.

Sharky seemed to have completely forgotten his earlier hostility toward Warren. "Say, young lad," he said, "I hear it was yer birthday yesterday. I say we celebrate the pirate way!"

He pulled a flute from his pocket and began playing a merry tune. More flutes emerged as other pirates joined in.

Before long, a jig had started. The pirates played other improvised instruments, tapping on logs and barrels as percussion and blowing into jugs like woodwinds. Even Mr. Friggs was drawn out from the confines of his library, though Beatrice was absent, still recovering inside.

Petula and Sketchy spun in a circle, twirling and dancing as the pirates cheered and clapped along. Warren sat on a barrel and sketched the two of them in his sketchbook. He wanted to always remember this moment.

"Ahh, what a lovely sketch," Mr. Friggs said, sitting down on a wooden crate.

"Thanks!" Warren said, blushing.

"Your father would be so proud, not just of your artistic abilities, but of the manager you have become. He would be pleasantly surprised to see how well you've managed the hotel at only twelve years of age!"

"Thirteen, now!" Warren reminded him.

"Of course," Mr. Friggs said, his smile faltering. "About that . . . " His voice trailed off and he fell so silent that Warren thought for a moment the elderly man had fallen asleep.

"Mr. Friggs?"

"Er, yes," Mr. Friggs said, "I have a gift for you. In fact, it's not from me. It's from your father."

Warren shut his sketchbook with a snap, his attention now fully upon his tutor.

"He was planning to give this to you when you turned eighteen, the age at which he would have handed over the reins to the hotel. I've thought long and hard and I think that, given the circumstances, he would agree that I should give it to you now."

"What circumstances?"

"Turning thirteen and . . . all that comes with it."

Mr. Friggs was acting strangely, but Warren was so excited to receive a gift from his late father that he barely noticed. His tutor reached into his pocket and pulled out a little box. He handed it to Warren.

Upon lifting the lid, Warren found a ring nestled on a velvet cushion. It was a gold band set with a domed sapphire on top. Visible through the gem was a "W" stamped at the bottom.

Warren's eyes grew wide as he took the ring and slipped it over his knuckle of his squat finger. It fit perfectly. Wearing something his father had once owned gave him goosebumps.

"It's wonderful!"

"It suits you well," Mr. Friggs said, smiling wanly.

Warren ran his fingers along the edge of the gemstone and found a little latch. When he pressed it, a small glass disk swung out from the side.

"What's this?" Warren asked.

"I believe it is a magnifying lens, called a loupe," Mr. Friggs said. "I imagine your father must have used it to examine the fine print in all the contracts and documents he worked with while he was the manager."

Warren raised the loupe to his eye, the curved glass distorting Mr. Friggs's face. It was rather funny to see the man's nose expand and his eyes shrink.

"Wow!" Warren giggled. "Thank you, Mr. Friggs! This is the best birthday gift ever!"

"Now, if you'll excuse me, I think I'll retire to my room," Mr. Friggs said, easing to his feet. "Goodnight."

Warren continued to stare at the ring. It looked so important, so official. He felt like a grown manager now, not just a boy.

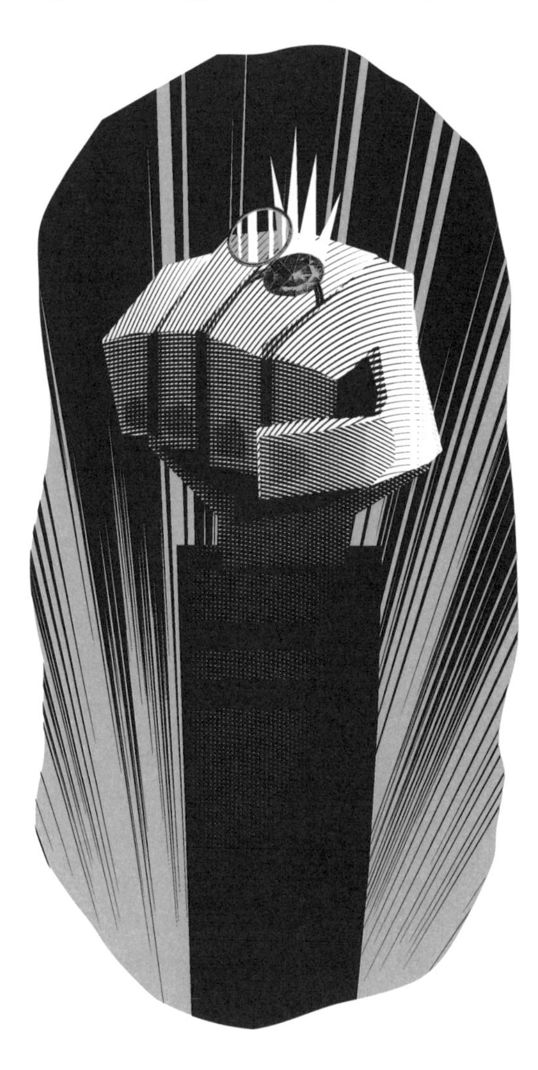

A rustling movement in nearby bushes drew his attention away from his gift. He could see a young face among the foliage, barely obscured by the leaves.

Bonny!

Warren's heart lurched in sympathy. She was watching the party from her hiding spot, no doubt sad to be excluded from the fun. She may have been a little difficult earlier, but Warren understood her predicament. She was just trying to be a good manager. He tucked his sketchbook in his pocket and hurried over. Bonny winced when she realized she had been discovered.

"It's O.K.," Warren said. "You don't need to hide. Please, join my party!"

"I don't want to! That's not why I'm here," Bonny said stubbornly. "I—I'm just checking on my pirates. They're my responsibility."

"I know. And I'm sorry we got off on the wrong foot," Warren said, holding out his hand. "I think we should be friends! I bet as the world's youngest managers we have a lot in common."

"I'm the youngest," Bonny insisted, though she accepted Warren's hand as he helped her to her feet.

"*And the smartest!*" screamed the parrot, still clinging to her shoulder. Warren grimaced. He had almost forgotten about the noisy bird.

He led Bonny over to the festivities. The pirates, who were all in good spirits, cheered when they saw her. Only then did she manage a small smile.

"Who invited her?" Petula said. She had finished her jig with Sketchy and was refreshing herself with a sip of tropical juice.

"I did. No one deserves to be left out," Warren said.

"Hmph."

"Don't be upset," Warren said, taking Petula's arm. "Tonight is about having fun! Now, let's join the others and dance!"

Petula smiled and let him pull her toward the dance ring. "I thought you'd never ask!"

TWEE...
TWEE...
TWEE...

TWEE?
TWEE...
TWEE
!!!!

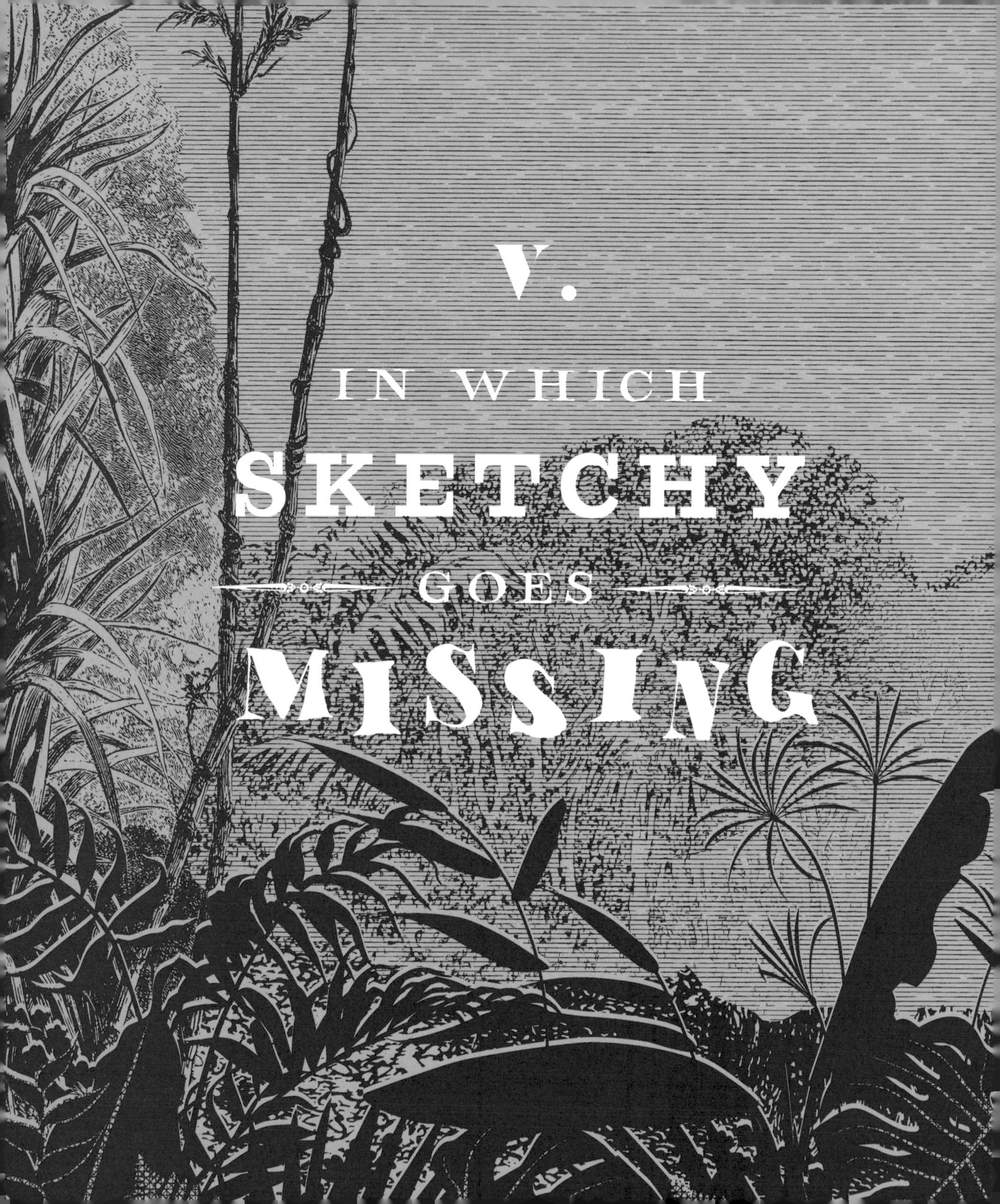

V.
IN WHICH SKETCHY GOES MISSING

he next morning, Warren stood on his freshly repaired roof and yanked on a rope, pulling his new flag up the mast. He admired his sparkling ring as the flag inched higher and higher. The hotel crows croaked appreciatively, being fans of shiny objects. When the flag reached the top, it flapped in the breeze, looking very official, indeed. It was the perfect finishing touch to his beloved hotel.

A cheer rose from the beach below and Warren waved to Petula and the pirates, who were squinting up into the morning sunlight. The party had gone rather late the night before, but they all looked well rested, thanks to Warren's signature hospitality. Warren would feel a little sad to see them all go. It was nice to have a hotel full of guests again, even if only for one night.

Using a rope, Warren rappelled down the side of the hotel and landed with a light thump upon the sand.

"Well, I suppose this is farewell!" he said, bowing respectfully to Captain Grayish-whitishbeard, Bonny, and the others. "Thank you for making my birthday so special."

"Yarr, whersh the Great Eight?" asked the toothless pirate. "We wanna pay our reshpecths!"

Warren looked around. Not seeing his tentacled friend, he yelled out, "Sketchy?"

There was no response. Petula frowned. "Where could it be?"

"I don't know," Warren said, a queasy feeling wriggling in his stomach. "I can't believe Sketchy isn't here to bask in the pirates' praise one last time."

"Oh, dear!" Mr. Vanderbelly said, rushing forward with his notebook ready. "We might have a scandal on our hands! I must document it!"

"Don't get ahead of yourself," Petula said. "Though, come to think of it, I don't remember seeing Sketchy at breakfast, which is very unusual."

"Nor did it help me prepare the morning's meal," Chef Bunion added. "I assumed it overslept after all the festivities last night. I'll go check the hotel." He hurried up the gangplank, calling for Sketchy.

A chill settled over Warren. He realized with horror, and a fair share of guilt, that he hadn't seen Sketchy since the night before. How had he managed to overlook his friend's absence all morning?

"I remember dancing with Sketchy at the party last night," Petula said. "But the rest is a blur."

Warren nodded, feeling numb. He, too,

was so busy dancing that he couldn't even say for sure when he had last seen Sketchy. Where could it have gone?

"Don't panic," Petula said. "This island isn't very big. Sketchy has to be somewhere!"

yelled Captain Grayishwhitishbeard. "Spread out! Comb the island! Don't stop until you find it!"

The pirates jumped into action, fanning out across the beach amid Bonny's protests. "Stop this at once!" she sputtered. "I'm the one in charge here, and we're going home! Let them worry about finding that creature!" But no one paid her any heed—the pirates were on a mission.

"Warren, look!" Petula said. "Those look like they could be Sketchy's tracks."

She was pointing to a distinctive wavy pattern in the sand that led into the jungle.

"Why would Sketchy go in there?" Warren asked, hurrying toward the foliage.

"Wait for me!" Mr. Vanderbelly cried, huffing and puffing after them.

As they entered the jungle, Warren could see Sketchy's tracks more clearly. It had snapped branches and pressed into the mossy jungle floor as it slithered along.

"There was a struggle!" Mr. Vanderbelly gasped, scribbling in his notebook.

"Don't get dramatic," Petula said with a sigh.

"No, he's right," Warren said. "Look."

He pointed to a section of foliage that was even more battered than the rest. Small trees had been pulled from their roots, and heavy tracks were gouged into the spongy ground.

"The trail continues over here!" Petula said.

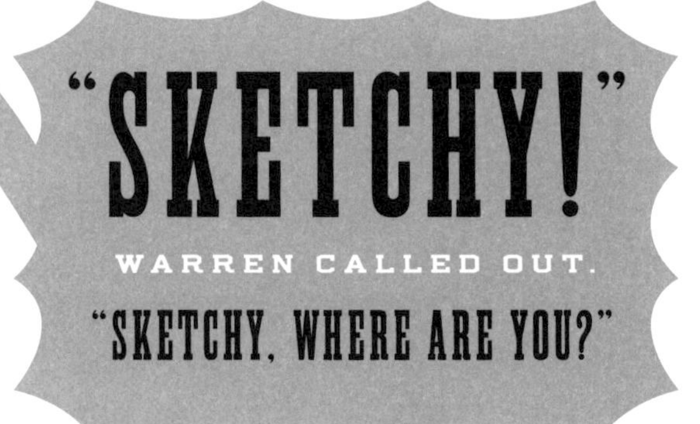

It seemed that something large had been dragged through the jungle. Gone were Sketchy's floppy prints; now, the foliage was completely flattened, as though a boulder had been dragged across it.

Warren and Petula ran faster and faster, following the tracks, as Mr. Vanderbelly struggled to keep up with them. Before long, they emerged on the windward side of the island. The beach was more rocky than sandy, but Warren could still make out the tracks heading in the direction of the water.

"The trail leads into the ocean," Warren observed. He noticed an indentation where a rowboat must have sat, and a chill ran down his spine.

"Sketchy wasn't alone." Petula pointed to a flute half buried in the gravely sand.

Warren picked it up and played a note. It made a shrill noise that sounded an awful lot like Sketchy's signature whistling.

Warren was filled with dread. "Someone lured it away. A pirate, by the looks of it."

"A KIDNAPPING!" Mr. Vanderbelly exclaimed with joy and horror.

"But who?" Petula asked. "All the pirates were at the party."

Warren sank to his knees in despair. Someone had kidnapped his beloved pet. Sketchy and its captor could be miles from the island by now, and he didn't even know which direction they had gone. The ring on his finger suddenly felt heavy on his hand. What kind of manager would lose his best friend? He didn't deserve such a precious gift.

By now, Captain Grayishwhitishbeard and the rest of the search party had arrived, panting and groaning about sore joints. For senior citizens, they certainly were resilient. Bonny trudged after them, looking irritable. Chef Bunion brought up the rear, shaking his head sadly. "Sketchy's not in the hotel. I'm sorry, Warren."

"Does anyone know who could have taken Sketchy?" Warren asked the assembled pirates. "We found a flute in the sand."

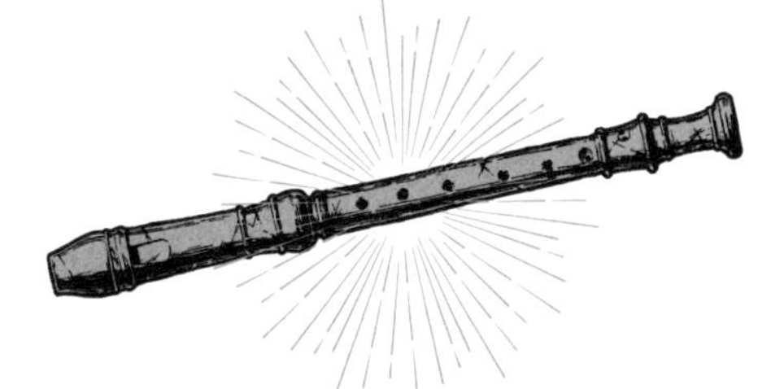

"You dare accuse MY pirates?" Bonny exploded. "My crew would never do such a thing!"

"They're not even that clever!" screamed her parrot.

"I'm not accusing anyone!" Warren cried. "I just want to find my friend. If anyone has any information, please . . . "

"Arr, lad," Sharky said gently. "We Calm Waves crew all be accounted for. It not be one of us, that's for sure."

"Sketchy could be anywhere by now," Warren said, looking out at the vast ocean. "How will I ever find it?"

"Arr, there may be someone that could help," Captain Grayishwhitishbeard said. "There be an old sea witch who lives underwater. She has a magic pearl that reveals lost things. I reckon she could show ye a glimpse of yer pet."

Bonny scoffed. "Witches can't be trusted. Everyone knows that."

"Excuse me?" Petula said. "You do realize I'm a witch, right?"

"Yeah, and I don't trust ya!" Bonny snapped.

"Please, don't argue," Warren said, stepping between them. "I'll go anywhere if I can find a clue to Sketchy's whereabouts. How do I find this sea witch?"

"I'll give ye the coordinates," Captain Grayishwhitishbeard said, "as long as ye let me join yer crew. I miss a life at sea, and that thar hotel is a fine ship."

"It's a deal!" Warren said. "We'd be honored to have you."

"Us, too!" the elderly pirates chimed in. "We want to help!"

"No! No! Absolutely not!" Bonny protested. "We are all going back to Calm Waves right NOW!"

"But Bonny! This be the Great Eight we're talking about!" Sharky said. "If it be in danger, we have a duty to save it!"

"No, we don't!" Bonny countered. "You are all retired, remember? Your adventuring days are over! You're too old to go back to sea!"

"Positively ancient!" screeched the parrot.

"Very well. You leave us no other choice." Sharky's face darkened and then he cried:

Bonny's eyes went as wide as saucers.

"No!"

"We're going, and thatsh that!" retorted the toothless pirate. "And Warren be our new captain!"

A cheer rose up: *"YAARRR!"*

The mob of old pirates charged back in the direction of the hotel, leaving Bonny in the dust. Warren hesitated, seeing the young girl's stricken expression.

"Come on, Warren," Petula said. "Let her be. She deserves it."

"No one deserves to be left alone," Warren said. "Especially on an island in the middle of nowhere."

Petula sighed. Warren did have a point.

"Bonny," Warren said, "please, come with us."

"But I can't abandon Calm Waves," Bonny said, her eyes shimmering. "It's my home."

"If there's one thing I've learned, it's that home is more than just a building," Warren said. "It's the people that live in it. As long as you have them near, you'll always be home."

"Wow, that's the corniest thing I've ever heard," Bonny said, and Warren blushed.

"Cue the violin!" the parrot squawked.

Bonny gave Warren a light sock in the arm. "Fine, I'll go, if only to keep those pirates in line. They may be old, but they're still a rowdy bunch."

"Welcome to the crew," Warren said. "Now, let's go find Sketchy!"

VI.
IN WHICH
WARREN
DIVES
DEEP

Warren sat with Mr. Friggs in his library, poring over the maps and coordinates that Captain Grayish-whitishbeard had given them.

"Hmmm," Mr. Friggs said, as he used a compass to measure angles across a faded map.

"Is the sea witch far?" Warren asked anxiously.

"Actually, her lair appears to be quite close," Friggs said. "We'll be there by day's end, I'd say, as long as the winds cooperate."

Warren sagged in relief. But there was still one problem. "Captain said the sea witch lives underwater. How will I be able to visit her? You don't think the hotel can turn into a submarine, do you?"

"Doubtful," Friggs said. "The hotel is made entirely of wood—not submarine material at all."

"I suppose you're right," Warren said.

"But fortunately, I do believe I have a solution." Mr. Friggs eased to his feet and hobbled across the room, picking his way around stacks of books and collectibles from his adventuring days: ancient sculptures, decorative gourds, antique furniture.

With a flourish, he yanked on a sheet covering a mound of items piled in the corner, sending dust motes swirling in the air. Through the haze, Warren spotted a taxidermied weasel wearing spectacles, a tattered picnic basket, and a somewhat spooky-looking ventriloquist dummy.

But those weren't the items Mr. Friggs was after. He rooted around in the pile and emerged with a rubbery suit attached to a bulbous helmet. A metal tank was strapped to the back, and a tube snaked its way around to the glass faceplate.

“A SCUBA SUIT!”

the old man announced. “Your grandfather, Warren the 11th, used it in his explorations when he was a young lad.”

“Wow!” Warren exclaimed. “But . . . will it still work?”

“I don’t see why not,” Friggs said. “It’s just a bit dusty, that’s all.”

“It looks a little big,” Warren said as Mr. Friggs handed him the suit. “And it’s really heavy!”

“You’ll feel light as a feather underwater,” Mr. Friggs said. “Go ahead and try it on.”

With his tutor’s assistance, Warren wriggled into the suit. It smelled like mildew, and the rubber felt cold against his skin, but as soon as he pulled the globe-shaped helmet over his head, he felt like a true adventurer! He could hardly wait to try it out underwater. Warren grinned at Mr. Friggs through the glass faceplate, but Mr. Friggs wore a grave expression on his face.

“Is everything O.K., Mr. Friggs?” Warren asked, pulling off the helmet.

“It’s just . . . I can’t help but worry.”

Warren smiled. "Well, I'd be worried if you weren't worried, Mr. Friggs!"

"I've been debating whether to tell you something. It might be complete nonsense, and not worth troubling you over."

Warren's smile faltered. "I want to know anyway," he said. "What is it?"

Mr. Friggs hesitated but knew he must tell his young charge: "The thirteen-year curse. I once dismissed it as a silly rumor, but given all the bad luck you've endured of late, I've begun to question whether it might in fact be real."

"Not you, too!" Warren cried. "I didn't think you were superstitious like Uncle Rupert!"

"I'm most certainly not!" Mr. Friggs sputtered, offended by the comparison. "At least, not usually. But in this case, there is a family legend that I've avoided telling you about. I didn't want to frighten you as a young boy. But I think you're old enough now to hear it, even if it turns out to be nothing more than make-believe."

Warren nodded grimly. "Go on."

"Very well. The legend goes that, during the Great War, Warren the 7th feuded with an evil witch who placed a curse upon the family. She called it the 'thirteen-year curse.' From the sound of it, one might think it would have lasted only thirteen years, but generations have passed and bad luck has plagued each Warren since. I believe it may be triggered by the very act of turning thirteen."

Warren felt queasy. It was just as he feared.

"Is there any way to break the curse?" he asked.

Mr. Friggs shook his head. "I'm afraid I don't know. Your grandfather perished trying to find a cure. As for your father, he rarely spoke of it, but he did mention that you would need the ring someday. That's why I decided to give it to you. If the curse is real, I think it might protect you."

Warren flexed his finger under the rubber

glove of the scuba suit. Even though he couldn't see the ring, he felt safer for having it on him.

"Keep it close," Mr. Friggs warned.

"I'll never take it off!" Warren promised.

⚓ ⚓ ⚓

the hotel approached a patch of dark, choppy water. Jagged rocks poked through the foam like enormous teeth. Warren used his periscope to carefully steer coming within inches of colliding with the treacherous obstacles.

"This is a suicide mission!" Bonny snapped. "Most ships never make it past these rocks. And this isn't even a proper ship, just some clunky old hotel!"

"Don't ye worry, Miss Bonny, Warren knows what he be doing," Captain Grayishwhitishbeard chimed in.

Warren wished he could ignore Bonny's words, but through the viewfinder, he could see the remnants of shipwrecks scattered across the ocean floor. Maybe she was right. Maybe it was foolish to think he could maneuver the hotel through this area unscathed. Especially if he really was cursed.

Turning the wheel as gently as possible, Warren eased around another cluster of sharp spires. There was a loud *SCRRRRAPE* as the hotel edged through a narrow channel. Warren gritted his teeth, fearing that they would get stuck. But suddenly the scraping ceased, and they emerged into a clearing.

Warren wiped the sweat from his brow. They'd made it!

"I knew you could do it!" Petula said.

"Hmmph," Bonny grunted. "Beginner's luck."

"STILL CURSED!"
shrieked her parrot.

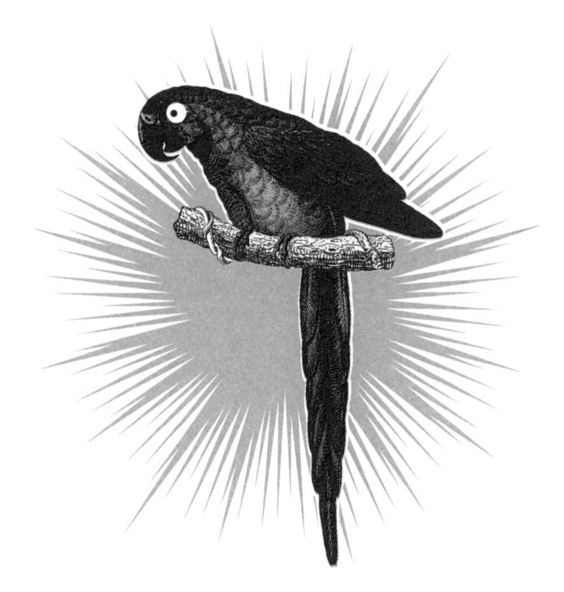

"How does he know about that?" Warren muttered.

"I told him," Rupert said cheerfully from his hammock.

"You're not cursed," Petula replied firmly.

"Actually . . . " Warren was about to tell Petula what Mr. Friggs had revealed, but thought better of it. He didn't want to worry her.

Warren checked the coordinates one last time and pulled a lever. The entire hotel shook as the anchor descended with a loud *CLANG!* He went over to the cockpit window and peered out, but the water was as dark as night.

"You're sure she's down here?" Warren asked Captain Grayishwhitishbeard doubtfully.

"YARR, THIS BE THE SPOT!"

he replied with confidence. "I visited her years ago meself."

"What had you lost?" Warren asked.

"I lost me foot," he replied gravely.

Warren glanced uneasily at the Captain's peg leg. His friend didn't elaborate, and Warren decided it was probably best not to question him further.

"Well, I suppose I better go find this sea witch," Warren said, changing the subject.

Grabbing his scuba suit, he led the way out of the control room and upstairs as Petula, Bonny, and Captain Grayishwhitishbeard followed behind. In the lobby, several of the elderly pirates were relaxing in the couches and armchairs, knitting stocking caps and socks and chatting. Even Beatrice had recovered enough to join them, sitting in a recliner sipping tea. They all paused to salute Warren as he entered. Warren blushed, surprised by the formality. It did feel rather nice to be treated like a real captain.

"Hey, I'm still your leader!" Bonny admonished them. "Don't forget that!"

The pirates grumbled and responded with a salute toward Bonny as well, but it was half-hearted at best.

"I'll be back soon!" Warren told them. *Hopefully*, he added silently, as he opened the front door and stepped onto the porch.

The waves churned, sending sprays of icy water onto the deck, and Warren shivered. With Petula's help, he pulled on the cumbersome suit, his heart beating with a mix of anticipation and anxiety.

Suddenly, a breathless Mr. Vanderbelly burst onto the porch, ready to document the action in his trusty notebook. "I'm just in time to witness brave young Warren as he descends into the fathomless deep to confront a dastardly witch!" he narrated in a dramatic tone of voice. "What dangers will he face?"

"Hopefully none," Petula declared. She sighed and added: "I wish I could go, too. Mom, do you know any spells that will let me breathe underwater?"

Beatrice smiled and shook her head. She pulled out a series of cards in rapid succession and Warren struggled to follow along. He caught a glimpse of an anchor, a boat, a rope, a shark, and, curiously, a slice of pie.

"She says you should tie a rope to your waist and tug on it if you need help," Petula said. "I can practice my rope magic by pulling you up quickly if you get into trouble."

"That's a great idea," Warren said.

"I still think this whole thing is a terrible idea," Bonny chimed in.

"Especially for someone who's cursed!" cried her parrot.

"I'll be fine," Warren said, more confidently than he felt.

"Yarr, take me cutlass." Captain Grayishwhitishbeard held out his blade. "In case you meet a shark!"

Warren grimaced. "Thank you, but I think I'll pass. I'm more likely to accidentally cut the rope—or myself—if I bring it along."

"Besides, your brain is your best weapon," Petula replied encouragingly. She fitted the helmet over Warren's head and locked it in place. "You've gotten out of worse scrapes by being clever."

“Thanks,” Warren said, his voice muffled and distant. He knew he was good at solving riddles, but he wasn’t sure that talent would help him in this situation.

He checked to make sure the rope around his waist was tied tight and that the other end was well secured to a nearby beam. He gave a thumbs-up to the group assembled on the porch and they returned the gesture. With a deep breath, Warren stepped off the deck and into the water.

For a moment, a dark froth of bubbles surrounded him, and Warren felt a bolt of fear as he sank like a stone.

But then the bubbles dissipated, and though the water was still black as ink, Warren could make out a school of tiny fish flitting this way and that, an amorphous undulating cloud. He steadied his breathing and drifted lower and lower, reminding himself to keep an eye out for danger.

Just when he was beginning to fear that he would continue sinking forever, he noticed a strange phosphorescent light illuminating the sandy ocean floor. He realized that the source was a patch of strange-looking underwater plants dancing in the current from where they grew among a cluster of porous rocks. The plants shone in a variety of colors—pink, green, and blue—and the multihued light they created was quite enchanting. Warren drifted closer, hypnotized. He was eager to touch one of the glowing fronds . . . they looked so soft and inviting.

Suddenly, the soothing colors shifted to a violent red, and tendrils shot out like spears. In the blink of an eye, Warren was wrapped from head to toe in vines. He could feel an electric current buzzing outside his diving suit. How grateful he was that it was made of rubber, which did not conduct electricity, or else he would have been fried like a crisp!

Warren let out a cry, but he knew it was hopeless. No one could hear him. Not all the way down here. He couldn't even reach his rope to tug on it. His arms were wrapped tightly at his sides. Angry red light flared around him as the tendrils wrapped tighter and pulled him deeper into their fold. Warren began to regret not bringing along Captain Grayishwhitishbeard's cutlass after all. How else would he free himself? He wriggled and thrashed as hard as he could, but the plants only seemed to further tighten their grip.

Then Warren recalled what Petula said about his mind being his best weapon. Was there a way to think himself out of this conundrum? Clearly, he couldn't reason with the plants. But he could stop panicking and start thinking logically.

This type of plant is likely used to electrocuting and eating fish, Warren thought. *Perhaps if I stop struggling and flopping around like a fish, it'll stop trying to shock me into submission.*

Warren allowed his body to go limp, and sure enough the electrical current ceased. Not only that, but the plants loosened their death grip as well.

It's working! Warren thought. *Maybe once it realizes I'm not edible, it will lose interest and let me go!*

He just needed to be patient. He continued playing dead as the plants' fronds explored the suit, searching for something to eat.

There was only one problem: it tickled!

Warren did his best to stay still and lifeless, but the curious poking and prodding

proved to be too much. His body jerked involuntarily as he burst into laughter: *"TEE HEE HEE!"*

Bubbles exploded from the exit valve on his tank, and the plant reared back as though alarmed. That was exactly what Warren needed. The plants let go just long enough for Warren to kick his feet and slip away.

"Ha!" he cried, triumphantly. But then to his horror, a single extra-long tendril shot out, seizing his ankle.

Warren kicked furiously, trying to avoid being pulled back into the deadly vines, but the plant was too strong and Warren was getting short of breath.

All of a sudden, a strange shape burst out from the sand and snapped the tendril in two. Warren was amazed to see a giant clam had just saved him! The plant retracted, flashing white.

"PTOOOOOH!" the clam said, spitting out the discarded tendril. "Those things taste terrible!"

It was a large clam, almost as big as Warren, with an opalescent ribbed shell and a single enormous eye.

"You saved me!" Warren said. "Thank you."

"Well, I thought you were a goner at first," the clam said. "There's nothing I can do against an entire nest of those sea vines. But I can take on one of 'em, that's for sure! The broken part will grow back, of course, but who can say how long it will take? Maybe a few hours. Maybe a few days. Maybe a few w—"

"Er, well, thanks again for your help," Warren interrupted. "But I'm actually in a bit of a hurry."

"Of course you are!" declared the clam. "I dare say that's why you got into trouble in the first place! The way I see it, the more you rush, the sloppier you get. You miss the little things. The details. The danger. Even I've been known to be guilty of that, yes, indeed! One time I was in quite a hurry. I can't remember for what now, but I'm sure it was important! Anyway, it was a murky day. Though all days down here tend to be murky—"

"Um, that sounds very interesting," Warren interrupted again, awkwardly edging away from the talkative clam. "But I have to go."

"Where are you going?" the clam asked, floating after him. "I can tell you my story along the way."

"O.K.," Warren said uneasily. "Well, I'm looking for the sea witch. You wouldn't happen to know where she is, would you?"

"Well, of course I know the sea witch!" the clam said, happy as a clam. "Everyone around here knows the sea witch! By golly, she created quite a stir when she first moved in around these parts. Most of us had never seen a human before, let alone a witch! I still remember the first time I laid eyes on her—"

"That's wonderful," Warren cut in, "but could you tell me where to find this sea witch? And as succinctly as possible?"

"Succinct!" the clam exclaimed. "I do love that word. You seem to have an impressive vocabulary for a boy your age. What a relief to engage in scintillating conversation with another intelligent being. As you might guess, a clam like myself doesn't have anyone interesting to talk to down here. Most fish are downright dull, if I do say so myself. Sharks, however, are more intelligent than they look, but they always want to eat me before we have a chance to chat!"

"The sea witch?" Warren prompted.

"Oh, yes, right this way! Follow me!" the clam said merrily, and it floated along, bobbing in the water while chattering on about this and that. Warren thought his ears might fall off, but he was still grateful to have someone to show him the way.

VII.
IN WHICH
WARREN VISITS
THE
SEA WITCH

efore long, Warren and his gregarious guide arrived at an underwater grotto, lush with colorful sea anemones and a garden of plants that looked far less threatening than the deadly vines Warren had recently encountered. The entire area glowed with the light of hundreds of phosphorescent fish swimming to and fro and nibbling at the vegetation. Warren could see a cave at one end, its opening shimmering eerily like one of Petula's portals.

"That's where you go in, right through there!" announced the clam.

"Great, thanks!" Warren said, eager to be rid of the chatty mollusk.

He quickly swam toward the entrance but then *BONK!* He ran into what felt like a pane of glass. Thankfully, his helmet protected his head from what would have been a nasty bump.

"Oops, sorry. I didn't get a chance to warn you about that," the clam said. "You didn't think a sea witch would let just anyone enter her cave, did you? There's a spell blocking the entrance."

"I can see that," Warren said. "You wouldn't happen to know how to break it, would you?"

"Well, of course I do! The sea witch entrusted me with the answer to the riddle that dissolves the barrier. It's really quite brilliant. Few people ever guess it."

"So, what's the riddle?" Warren asked impatiently.

"Oh! Yes, of course. Right this way."

The clam led Warren to a nearby clearing in the sand where several colorful seashells were arranged in a pattern.

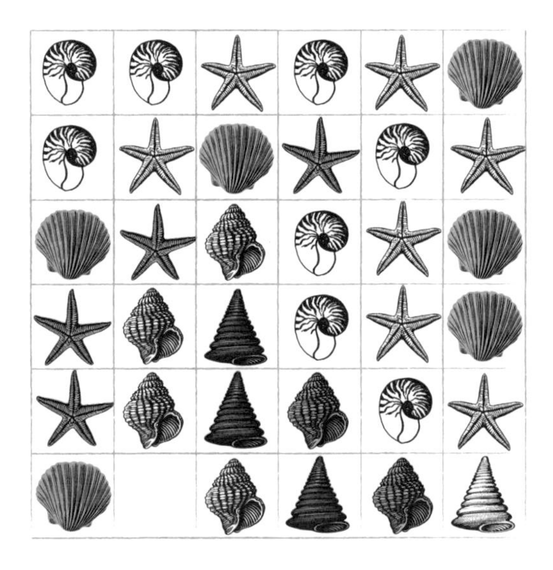

"Your job is to determine which shell belongs in the empty space," the clam said. "You get one chance. But don't worry—if you're wrong, you can spend the day with me instead of that old witch!"

Hearing this only made Warren more anxious to get it right. He studied the arrangement closely, trying to figure out the pattern.

"I wish I could give you a hint!" the clam said. "I think it would be a lot nicer if I could help visitors just a little bit, you know? But the witch doesn't want too many people getting it right, which is why she makes it so hard. But if it were me—"

"I'm sorry," Warren interrupted, "but could I please have a little quiet while I concentrate?"

"Oh, sure! Silence is golden, as they say. Though why they chose gold and not silver or even blue, I'm not really sure. Just because gold is expensive doesn't mean it's necessarily the best color. Personally, green is my favorite—"

Warren did his best to tune out the talkative clam as he studied the pattern further. He soon realized that each shell's position depended on the shells on either side. White nautilus shells and blue seashells had a white starfish between them. Blue starfish and blue cone shells had a white conch shell between them.

"That's it!" Warren said as he bent down to pick up a blue starfish and place it in the empty spot. "A blue seashell and a white conch shell always have a blue starfish between them, which means that's the only thing that can fit here!"

"Wow!" the clam said. "I must say I'm mightily impressed. You solved it even quicker than the last person, and that was years ago!"

There was a shimmer as the magical barrier blocking the cave entrance dissipated into thousands of tiny bubbles.

"Thanks, and goodbye!" Warren said, eager to be on his way.

"Unfortunately, I can't follow you inside—you'll see why. But I'll be waiting here when you come out," the clam said. "We still have so much to talk about!"

"Wonderful," Warren muttered.

Stepping through the opening of the cave was like walking through a large soap bubble. Warren quickly realized why the clam couldn't follow—the sea witch had cast another spell on this place, sealing it from water and filling it with air that was uninhabitable by aquatic creatures. No longer weightless, as he had been in the water, Warren stumbled under the sudden weight of his diving suit.

He recovered quickly and proceeded into a winding stone tunnel that was engraved with magical glyphs and lit by torches. The tunnel eventually led to a doorway across which hung a crystal-beaded curtain.

Warren pulled off his helmet and parted the curtain uncertainly. "Hello?"

"Come in," a whispering voice beckoned.

Warren swallowed nervously and stepped into a small circular room. It glowed orange from the light of a fire, upon which a cauldron bubbled with a pungent-smelling fish stew. An ancient-looking woman with bluish leathery skin and inky black hair hunched nearby, seated upon a pile of pillows in front of a luminous pearl that was as big as Warren's helmet.

"Come forward," the sea witch whispered. "I don't bite."

She grinned and Warren saw that her teeth looked like Sharky's—they were sharpened into tiny points, giving her a feral appearance.

"Um, hello," Warren said, approaching her nervously. "I've come to seek your help. You see, I've lost something—someone—very important to me, and I'm hoping you can help me find it."

"Sit," the sea witch hissed, and Warren obeyed.

"Knowledge comes at a price," she said in her whispering voice. "To find something precious, you must lose something precious. What do you offer me for my magic?"

She held out her bony hands, awaiting an offering.

Warren's thoughts instantly flew to the precious ring around his finger. He couldn't give her that—especially if it helped protect him from his curse!

Warren had to fib. "I—I don't have anything!" he said. "Can I offer you some

work instead? I can tidy up your place, or fix anything that might be broken."

"You do have something," the sea witch hissed. "I can sense it." Warren curled his hands in his glove, feeling the ring tighten around his finger. How upset would Mr. Friggs—and his father!—be if he were to give it up so easily? But Sketchy was worth a hundred heirloom rings.

Warren swallowed hard and began to reach for the ring. But then he stopped. He realized that he had something else to offer: his beloved sketchbook, tucked, as always, in his back pocket. That was just as precious as his ring. He had to decide between the two or return to the hotel empty-handed.

"Well?" the witch prompted. "If you aren't willing to pay the price, then you must leave."

Warren had made his decision. He nodded sadly and unzipped his suit to reach the sketchbook. He would always have his artistic talents, but the ring was irreplaceable. Even so, it was painful to hold his sketchbook and flip through it one last time. Drawn on its pages were landscapes, fanciful illustrations, and portraits of his friends, including the sketch he had made of Petula dancing with Sketchy just the night before. But the most heart-wrenching of all was seeing the drawings done by Sketchy's own tentacles depicting their adventures together. They were childlike, but Warren knew they were done with love.

Warren reminded himself that he would rather have Sketchy back than these drawings. After all, once they were reunited, they could start a whole new sketchbook together! This thought heartened him and he was finally able to hand over his offering. The witch's gnarled hands closed over the book, and Warren let out a cry as it turned to sparkling dust. She sprinkled the dust over the pearl and chanted:

Ancient pearl of the ocean deep

Be my eye and help me seek

That which is lost
and must be found

With this offering,
you are bound!

Warren stared in amazement as the pearl began to throb. Its ghostly light seemed to permeate the room, blotting out even the fire's flames with a misty glow.

As Warren stared, the pearl's opaque surface turned shiny and mirror-like. With a gasp, he saw an image move across its surface. He leaned forward, straining to make sense of what it was.

TWEEE . . .

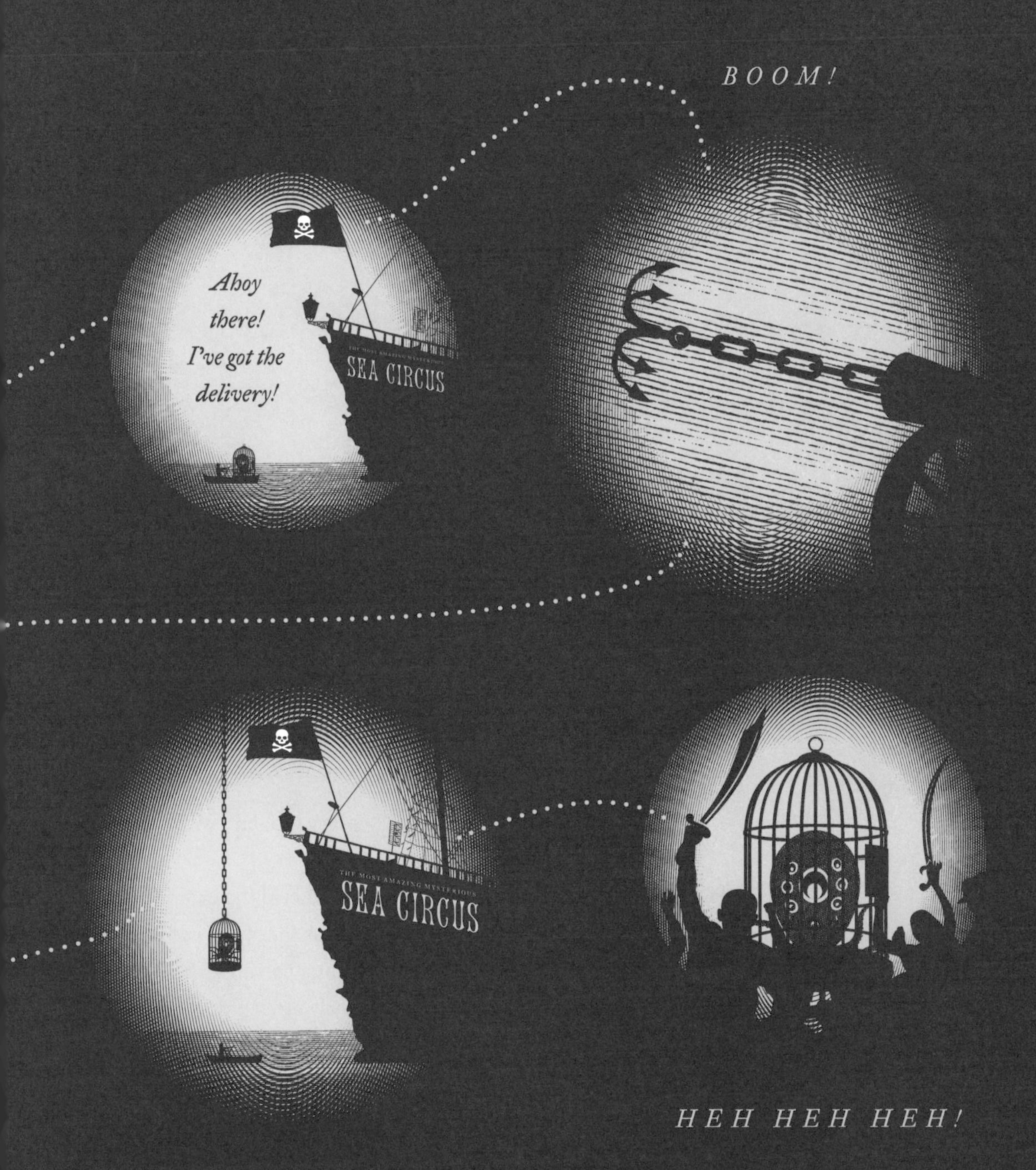
Ahoy there! I've got the delivery!
SEA CIRCUS
BOOM!
THE MOST AMAZING MYSTERIOUS
SEA CIRCUS
TWEEE...
HEH HEH HEH!

"Leave Sketchy alone!" Warren cried as the image in the pearl began to fade.

The pearl went dark, and the mysterious light in the room vanished.

"Please, bring it back!" Warren pleaded with the sea witch. "I still don't know where Sketchy is!"

"The pearl only reveals what is lost, not where it is lost," the sea witch replied, and her shoulders began to shake as a rasping voice escaped her lips. She was laughing at him!

Warren trembled with anger. He very rarely got angry. As manager of a hotel, he often had to keep a cool head when dealing with demanding guests, but in this instant, his emotions took over.

"You should be ashamed of yourself!" Warren sputtered. "Taking advantage of those who need help!"

The witch only replied with more mocking laughter.

Warren stormed toward the exit. He was so flustered, he almost forgot to put on his helmet before stepping through the bubble that separated the cavern's entrance from the water.

The talkative clam was in Warren's face almost instantly. "How'd it go?! Did you say hi for me? Did she remember me? Did you

find what you were looking for? You were in there for quite some time, I admit I began to get a little worried. Not that worried, but you can never be too careful—"

"I saw *what* I was looking for, but I still don't know *where* it is!" Warren said huffily. "Oh, that is a shame," the clam said, and for a moment it actually seemed at a loss for words.

Warren was too upset to notice, however. He yanked hard on the rope around his waist, signaling that he was ready to return to the surface. He felt a tug in response, and knew that Petula was using her rope magic to rein him in.

"Hey, where're you going?" the clam asked, floating after him as Warren began to make his ascent. "There's still so much we can talk about!"

"Back home, and back to square one," Warren replied, glumly.

VIII.

IN WHICH WARREN DISCOVERS AN INVISIBLE CLUE

ack in the hotel lobby, Warren pulled off his helmet and wiggled out of his scuba suit, leaving a puddle on the floor.

"So, the young Warren has returned with nary a shark bite and all his limbs intact!" Mr. Vanderbelly announced, sounding perhaps a trifle disappointed.

"How did the old suit hold up?" Mr. Friggs asked.

"Very well, indeed," Warren said, thinking of how it had saved him from electrocution.

"Did you figure out where Sketchy is?" Petula asked anxiously.

"Well? Did you?" Bonny cut in.

"Not quite," Warren said. "But I did see it being delivered to a Most Amazingly Mysterious Sea Circus. Has anyone ever heard of such a thing?"

A loud clamor rose in the lobby as all the elderly pirates spoke at once.

"Arr! One at a time!" Captain Grayishwhitishbeard admonished them.

"Yarr, it be our greatest dream to visit the famous sea circus!" Sharky said.

"You're too old for that nonsense!" Bonny snapped. "Circuses are for kids!"

"Doeshn't mean we don't like to try each week!" the toothless pirate said.

"What do you mean, try each week?" Warren asked.

"Ignore them, it's all a bunch of silliness," Bonny said, folding her arms.

"UTTER FOOLISHNESS!" her parrot cried.

"Now, now, Bonny, he needs all the information he can get if he's to find his best mate," Captain Grayishwhitishbeard said, and he nodded at Sharky to continue.

"Yarr, a puzzle be printed in the weekly pirate paper, the *Privateer Post*. The solution hints at where the circus will be next. Only the smartest folk can find it!"

"A puzzle!" Warren cried. "That's perfect! Does anyone have a copy of the *Privateer Post*?"

"Right here!" One of the elderly pirate ladies hobbled over, waving a tattered paper in the air.

"Arr, we couldn't even solve this one," Sharky said. "Maybe you can!"

Everyone crowded around as Warren spread the paper upon the lobby's front desk. He flipped to the last page, which had some pirate cartoon strips and a review of a pirate silent film called *Dancing the Plank*.

The puzzle was in the bottom right corner.

THE MOST AMAZINGLY MYSTERIOUS

SEA CIRCUS

PUZZLE OF THE WEEK

Solve the puzzle to discover the Sea Circus's next location. Only the cleverest will succeed!

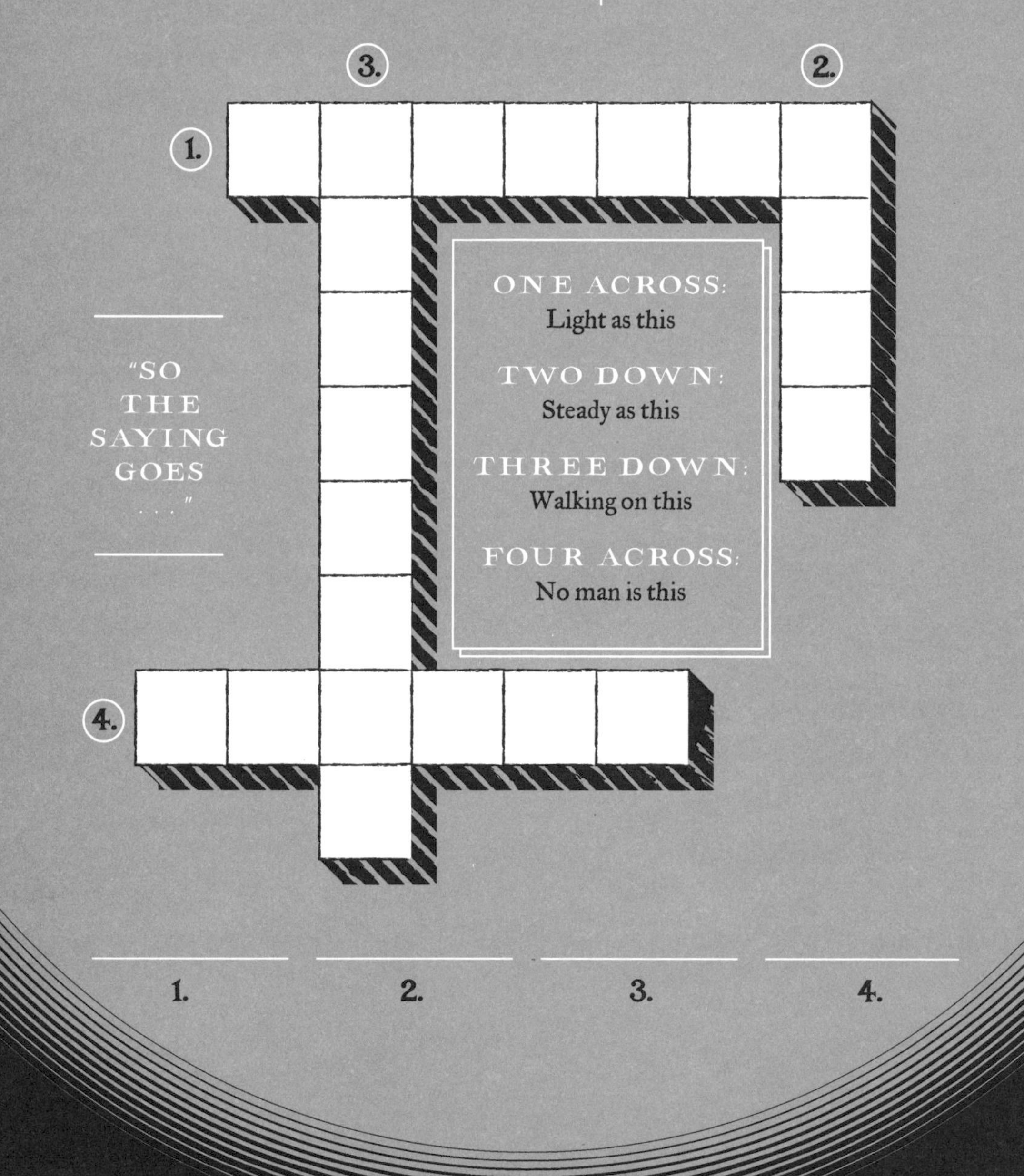

Leaning over Warren's shoulder, the group held its collective breath as he penciled letters in the boxes, solving one riddle at a time. Finally, he cried, "I've got it! The answer is Feather Rock in the Eggshell Islands! That's where Sketchy is! We should leave right away!"

The pirates let out a rowdy cheer.

"There's only one problem," Petula said. She pointed at the upper corner of the paper.

Warren looked crestfallen when he saw the date. "This paper is almost five weeks old."

"The Sea Circus is long gone from Feather Rock," Bonny said. "Obviously."

"Does anyone have a current paper?" Warren asked.

The pirates exchanged sheepish looks and coughed nervously.

"Arr," Sharky said, rubbing the back of his head, "the paper is delivered by bottle, you see, so it usually arrives a wee bit late. We solve the puzzles for fun more than anything. The truth be, Bonny's right: none of us will ever visit the Sea Circus. We be too old for such a folly."

"That's not true!" Warren said. "You will get to see the Sea Circus . . . because I'll take you there!"

The pirates cheered.

Warren looked down at the paper and sighed. "Though, I suppose it is a bit hard if we don't have a current paper to work with."

"Where can we find one?" Petula asked, glancing at Bonny.

"Don't ask me!" the pirates' leader replied tartly. "I think this whole idea is ridiculous."

"Yarr, there be a place nearby that'll have yer paper, though it be a rough town for a youngun like you," Captain Grayishwhitishbeard said. "It be a pirate city called Scurvyville."

The pirates in the room gasped.

"That'sh where I losht me teesh!" Toothless cried.

"I once got into a fight there . . . and lost!" cried another.

"I was swindled out of me finest clothes," cried a third, "and I had to walk about wearing a barrel!"

"Like I said, it be a rough-and-tumble place," Captain added. "A place for thieves and charlatans. It be the place where pirates from all over the seas come to do business and get rowdy."

"But I'll find a current issue of the *Privateer Post* there?" Warren asked.

"That ye will. And hot off the presses, for it be printed there," Captain said, nodding.

"Oh, we must go!" Mr. Vanderbelly cried. "I love seeing where other papers are printed. Besides, I must keep an eye on my competition!"

"You'll be eaten alive in Scurvyville," Bonny announced to Warren. "It's a dirty and dangerous place. There are plenty of other, nicer towns where you can find a current issue."

"But they'll be farther away," Warren said. "And we don't have any time to lose!"

"Oh, come on. A smartypants like you can figure something else out," Bonny said, her arms folded against her chest.

"ANYTHING ELSE!" her parrot squawked.

Warren hesitated. Was he putting his crew in danger by venturing someplace so infamous? Still, he couldn't shake the image of Sketchy being hauled onto a circus ship. He had to hurry!

"I appreciate the thought," Warren said to Bonny, "but this is the fastest way, and Sketchy needs our help. Mr. Friggs? Can you get me the coordinates to Scurvyville? We set sail immediately!"

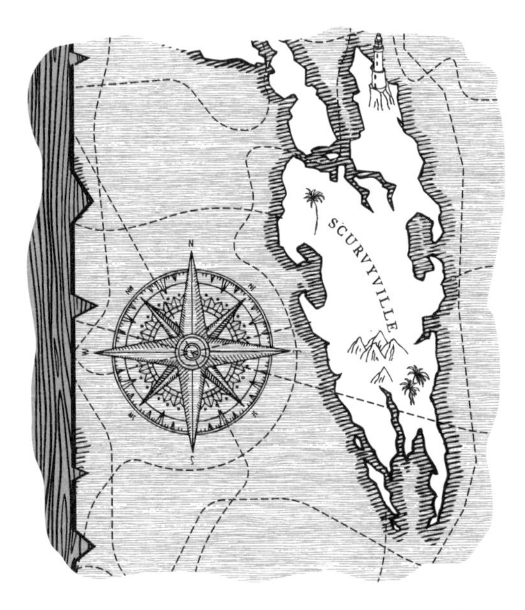

Despite Scurvyville being the closest town on the map, it was still a two-day journey to reach it. Fortunately, the seas were calm and the winds were blowing in the right direction to give them a much-needed boost.

Warren was impatient to arrive, but he busied himself with one of his favorite tasks: hospitality. Having a hotel full of elderly pirates ensured that he was kept on his feet from morning to night. There were special dietary requests, complaints of lumpy mattresses, lost hook hands, and the occasional missing set of dentures. Warren also had to contend with the many squabbles over the plush armchairs in the viewing parlor, as well as bickering over what music to play on the Victrola. Fortunately, Beatrice had recovered enough to play her violin, and her soothing tunes lulled them all into peaceful moods.

Warren took advantage of the temporary calm to pay a visit to his father's portrait.

"Thank you for the ring, Father," he said. "I know you meant for me to receive it when I turned eighteen, so I hope you don't mind me having it a few years early. Mr. Friggs thought it might help protect me in case I really am cursed."

Warren felt a sadness settle over him. "Were you cursed, too, Father? Is that why you died? But why didn't the ring protect you?"

The portrait did not answer, and Warren sighed. He would never have all the answers he craved. His eyes roamed over the familiar brushstrokes that formed the likeness of his father. He was always amazed by how so many random blotches of paint could create something so warm and lifelike. Being an artist himself, one of Warren's favorite pastimes was to study the techniques of painters who had come before him. He flipped the latch on his ring, exposing the loupe. Now he could observe the paintings in even greater detail.

He held the glass up to his eye and peered at his father's portrait. He gasped! Golden numbers shimmered on the surface of the canvas where none had been before.

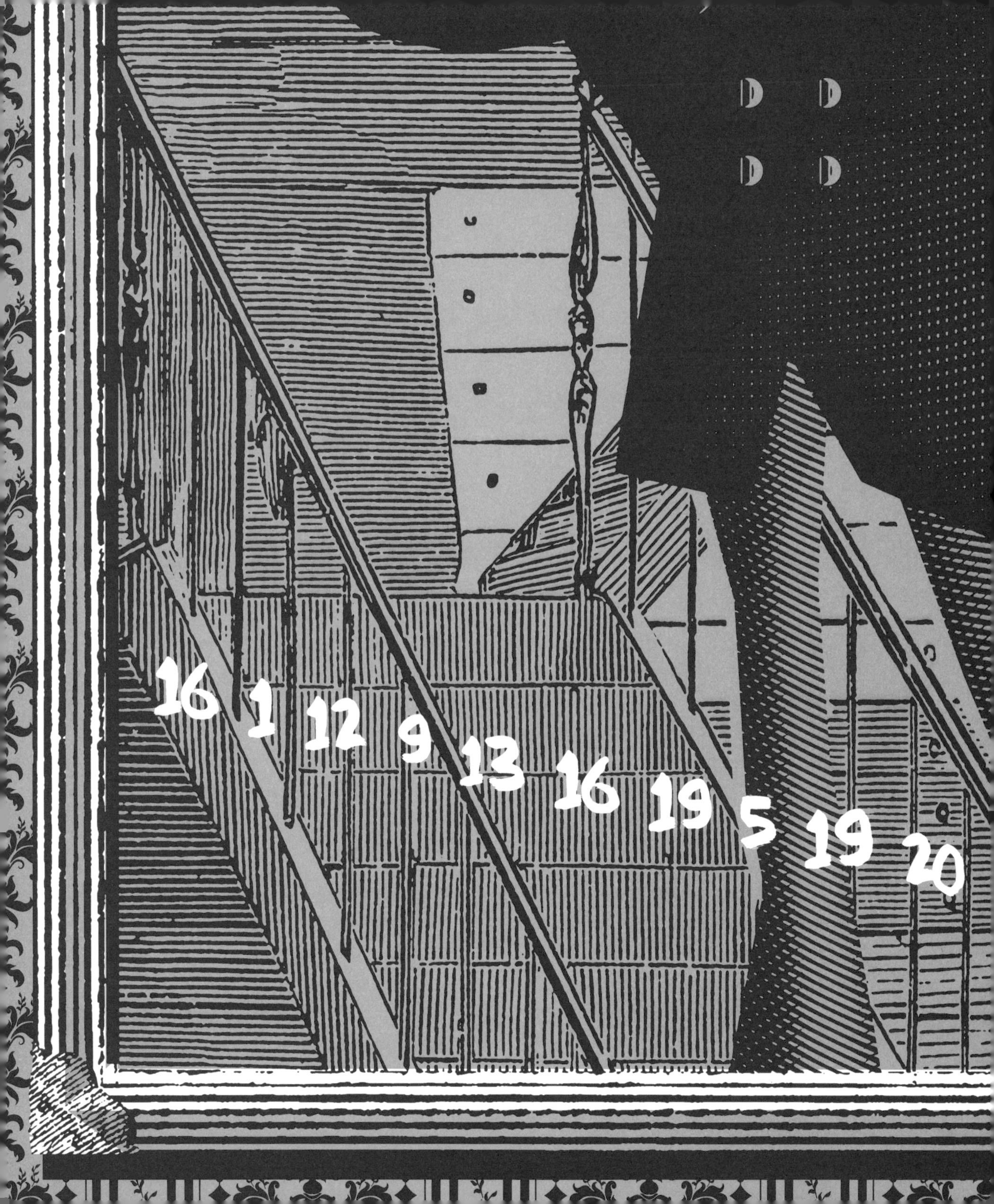
16 1 12 9 13 16 19 5 19 20

Warren pulled away the lens and stared at the painting with his bare eyes. The numbers vanished. He looked through the lens once more and the row of numbers reappeared across his father's portrait.

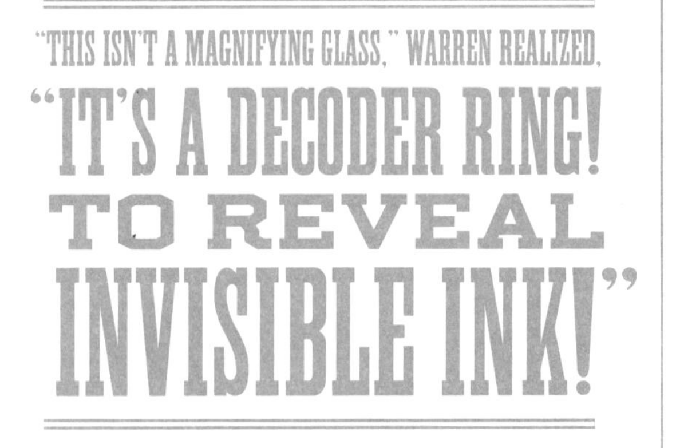

Warren quickly ran down the length of the portrait gallery, holding the glass lens to his eye, looking for more hidden figures. But there were none to be found. What could the string of numbers mean? Instinctively, he reached for his sketchbook but then remembered he no longer had one. Instead he wrote the numbers along his arm in ink.

"I better go see Mr. Friggs."

⚓ ⚓ ⚓

Mr. Friggs's library was a jumble of books, artifacts, and memorabilia, but it was the sort of jumble that made sense, at least to Mr. Friggs. The library Warren walked into now was not so much a jumble as a war zone. Everything was in complete disarray—books and objects were upended and askew, as though a hurricane had landed and tossed everything about.

"Mr. Friggs!" Warren cried out, alarmed. "Where are you? Are you all right?"

He could hear a muttering coming from the far left corner, so Warren made his way in that direction, climbing over a mound of crockery and tribal masks that lay over a smaller mound of rolled-up maps and tattered manuscripts.

Finally, he spotted Mr. Friggs, knee deep in a pile of wicker baskets and mechanical gears and coils. The old man was tugging at his sideburns and looked very distraught.

"Mr. Friggs? What happened?"

"I can't find anything!" Mr. Friggs sputtered. "I must be losing my mind!"

"Come sit at your desk and rest a moment," Warren said, leading his tutor to his favorite chair. He had to sweep away a pile of handwoven tapestries and a bag of chess pieces before the man could sit. Mr. Friggs groaned as he sank into his chair.

"I'll help you find whatever it is you're looking for," Warren said. "Maybe we can tidy up the place and get it more organized?"

This had always been one of Warren's private goals, but Mr. Friggs was reluctant to let him rearrange the library in any way.

"My navigational tools," Mr. Friggs said, his eyes still darting around the room. "I was just using them yesterday to chart the course to Scurvyville, and now I can't find them anywhere! They were on my desk, I'm certain. We won't be able to go anywhere accurately without them!"

"I'm sure they're around here somewhere," Warren said. "Try not to worry." Inside, though, Warren was more than a little concerned. The missing tools would delay their search for Sketchy.

"In the meantime, I have something I wanted to show you," Warren said, hoping a change of subject would ease his tutor's mind. He rolled up his sleeve to expose the numbers on his arm. "Do these numbers mean anything to you?" he asked. "I found them written in invisible ink on my father's portrait. The ring revealed them."

"Is that so!" Mr. Friggs said, pleased by a new puzzle to distract him from his troubles. "Perhaps it's some sort of passcode?"

"Or maybe it's coordinates!"

"There's too many numbers for that," Mr. Friggs mused. "Let me jot these down and see if I can figure out a pattern. Perhaps if we add them together..." Lost in thought, Mr. Friggs began scribbling equations on a fresh sheet of paper.

Warren let him be and hurried down to the control room. He wanted to try the numbers on the keypad and see if anything happened. But when he punched the keys of the typewriter, an angry *BUZZZZZ!* sounded as the control room alarm went off. A piece of paper shot out of a nearby slot, the word "INVALID" printed on its surface in red ink.

The noise was loud enough to wake even Uncle Rupert, who ran for the door, yelling, "I'm late for school!"

"Ooops, I guess that's not it," Warren said, frantically trying to stop the alarm. "I better think of something else!"

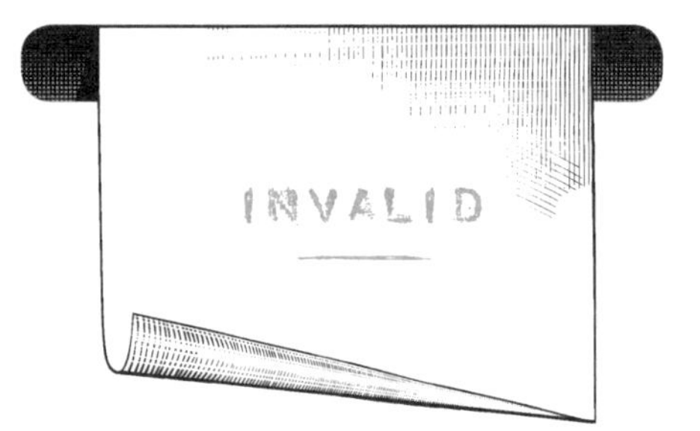

Tweee?
CREAK...
Well, hello old friend.
Tweeeee...
I admit, I never thought I'd see the likes of you again! You've certainly grown a lot. DID YOU MISS ME?
TWEEE!

Heh heh heh. Well, I won't make the mistake of letting you out of my sight again. After all these long years of searching, you're the key to finally luring the **GREAT EIGHT** *out of hiding... and once I find it, its caverns full of treasure* **WILL BE MINE!**

TWEEE!

That's right. So if you ever wish to see it again, you better cooperate.

But in the meantime, we have a show to put on. So you better start practicing!

Tweeee...

IX.

IN WHICH WARREN VENTURES INTO SCURVYVILLE

The hotel arrived at Scurvyville a full day later than expected, due to Mr. Friggs's missing instruments. The old man had finally agreed to allow Warren to tidy up the library as he continued to puzzle over the mysterious numbers, and even though Warren organized everything splendidly, the navigational tools were never found. What could have happened to them?

Fortunately, Captain Grayishwhitishbeard had an intuitive talent for sea navigation, and he helped guide them on the right course through the power of his memory alone. Before long, the port could be seen on the horizon, through a thick haze of smog.

"Land ho!" Captain Grayishwhitishbeard announced from the cockpit, where he was peering through the periscope.

"Great work, Captain!" Warren said.

The door to the control room swung open and Mr. Friggs entered, looking gleeful.

"What brings you all the way down here?" Warren asked.

"Good news, my boy! I cracked the code!"

"You did?" Warren grinned. "How?"

"I realized that it's not a mathematical puzzle. It's a word puzzle! Each number corresponds to a letter of the alphabet. A equals 1, B equals 2, C equals 3, and so on."

Mr. Friggs handed Warren a paper inscribed with the numbers from his father's portrait. Warren grabbed a pen and quickly wrote down the letters that corresponded with the numbers.

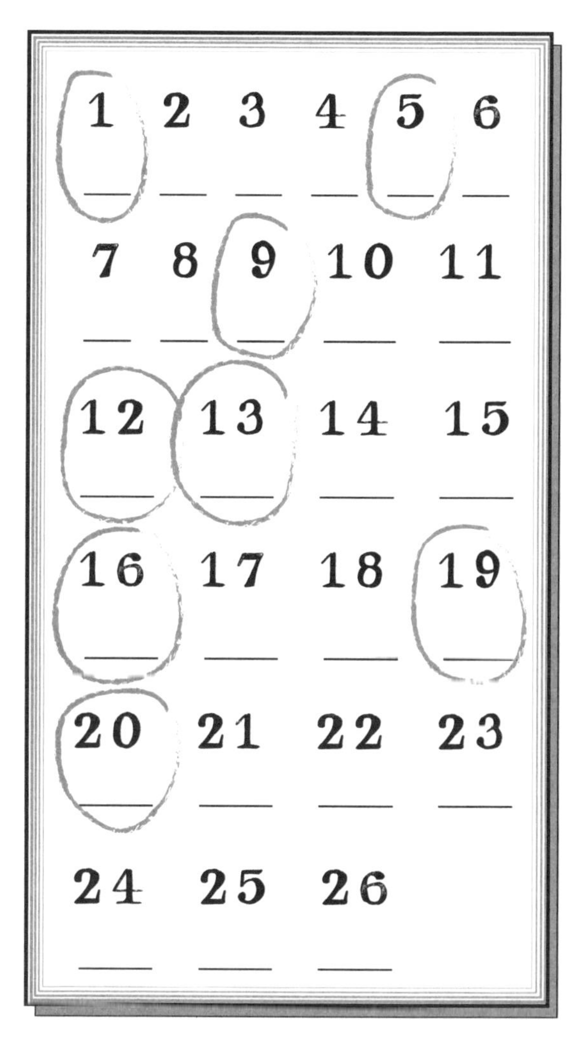

16 1 12 9 13 16 19 5 19 20

"Palimpsest?" Warren sounded out the word. "What does that mean?"

"It refers to a manuscript or page that has been written over or erased to make way for new writing," explained Mr. Friggs. "Traces of the old writing sometimes remain and are able to be recovered."

"Interesting," Warren said. "But why would that word be written over my father's portrait?"

"I'm afraid I have no idea," Mr. Friggs admitted. "But I would start looking around for palimpsests if I were you. I'll poke through my library and see if I can find any there."

"Thank you, Mr. Friggs," Warren said gratefully. "You did a great job solving this puzzle."

"Arrgh, sorry to interrupt," Captain Grayishwhitishbeard said as the hotel pulled into the docks. "But we've arrived at Scurvy-ville!"

The thick brown smog clung to the air, smelling of gunpowder and smoke. The sounds of booming cannons and firecrackers could be heard in the distance, as well as the occasional scream or peal of laughter. Trash littered the streets and the brightly painted ramshackle buildings were crammed close together, practically on top of one another, creating a haphazard tapestry of hues.

Warren hopped onto the wooden dock with Captain Grayishwhitishbeard, and they secured the hotel to a post with a thick rope so that it wouldn't drift away. Warren couldn't help but notice several pirates on the boardwalk, eyeing the hotel hungrily.

"Arr, there might be a bit o' trouble," Captain Grayishwhitishbeard said in a low voice. "Some of that lot might get the bright idea to try to take over the hotel. But don't ye worry, I'll guard it along with the rest of the Calm Waves crew."

"Thanks," Warren said, though he felt a little uneasy. Luckily, Beatrice had made a full recovery and was currently perched in the rooftop crow's nest serving as lookout. She was wearing a black cloak and looked rather like a crow herself. As he glanced up, she gave Warren a little salute, and he nodded back. Between her and his pirate guests, he knew the hotel was in good hands. Even so, the less time they spent in Scur-vyville, the better.

Petula walked out onto the dock, looking annoyed as Bonny followed on her heels. Mr. Vanderbelly hurried after them.

"I'm ready to go when you are," she said to Warren. "But I think they ought to stay behind."

"I know how to deal with unruly pirates," Bonny declared. "You guys will be swindled silly without my help!"

"YOU BETTER BELIEVE IT!" her parrot screeched.

"And I simply must see where the *Privateer Post* is printed!" Mr. Vanderbelly insisted. "How else am I supposed to steal— er, study their methods?"

Warren looked at Petula and shrugged. "Safety in numbers, I suppose, right?"

The unlikely foursome made their way from the harbor into the city. The buildings closed in around them, and suspicious eyes peered at them from every window. They weaved through narrow winding alleys, looking nervously over their shoulders as Scurvyville pirates leered at them with nasty grins or hostile sneers.

"Where do you suppose the printing press is?" Warren whispered to Bonny. "Should we ask for directions?"

"Not unless you want to be led into a trap!" Bonny said. "The only way to get information is to bribe someone. Watch."

Bonny walked up to a pirate leaning unsteadily against a large barrel. "You there!" she said, pulling out a shiny gold coin. "I'll give you this if you show us where the *Privateer Post* is. And I'll give you another if you do it quickly."

The pirate's eyes went wide at the sight of the coin and he licked his lips hungrily. "Arright, lassie," he said, holding out his hand. "Hand it over and I'll show ye the way!"

"Nice try!" Bonny said. "But I'm not giving you anything until you deliver the goods."

"He said hand it over," snarled a rough voice behind them. "Plus whatever else you have in your pockets."

Warren and his friends turned to see that they were surrounded by pirates. They had emerged from the shadows of the alleyway and began closing in, hands on their belts where their cutlasses hung.

"Great," Petula whispered. "We just managed to attract attention by flashing money around."

Bonny went pale. "Er, hold on, fellas . . . "

Warren knew he had to think fast. He grabbed the coin from Bonny's hand and threw it as hard as he could. "If you want it—go get it!" he cried.

The pirates stumbled over one another as they raced to reach the loose coin first.

"Run!" Warren cried, and they bolted in the opposite direction, not stopping until they emerged into a crowded plaza swarming with still more pirates.

As they paused to catch their breath, Mr. Vanderbelly sniffed the air. "I do believe I smell ink. Follow me!"

UTS
SALE
FREE TEST
2.5

He led them across the plaza and into a vibrant market crammed with stalls where pirate merchants were selling a dizzying array of wares. There were baskets of fruits, spices, tea leaves, and coffee beans. Tables were laden with silverware, silk, jewelry, tools, and trinkets. A baker was selling tins of "scurvy-proof" biscuits, and a weaver offered handmade flags in custom combinations. At yet another booth, a doctor sold medicine for seasickness and dropsy. There was a stall piled high with wooden toys for pirate children, and a tent filled with knives and other weapons, which was guarded by an exceptionally large woman and her black hound. There was even a stall selling parrots in every color of the rainbow; they flapped their wings to display their plumage. All their squawking was lost amidst the clamor of barter as pirate patrons negotiated for the best prices.

Warren's jaw dropped. He had never experienced any place like this. It was so vibrant, so chaotic!

"Try a taste of these delicious tropical pears, young master!" A young woman smiled at Warren, holding out a tray of peach-colored slices. Warren reached out to take one, but Bonny quickly swatted his hand away.

"That's a scam!" she said. "The minute you touch it, you own it. And then she'll make you buy the whole crate!"

The woman snarled as Bonny pulled Warren away from the booth. "Don't touch nothin'!" she warned.

"Aha!" Mr. Vanderbelly exclaimed as they exited the market. "I can definitely smell the printing press now!"

Even Warren could detect an acrid scent wafting in the air. The reporter quickened his pace and the rest followed when he turned right, then left, then right again, as though he were a bloodhound on a trail. They took yet another turn and finally there it was: an enormous brick building with rooftop smokestacks pumping out noxious plumes of black smog. Grimy gold letters hanging over the double doorway spelled out "The Privateer Post." Clanging and banging could be heard from within.

"You found it!" Warren said happily.

He stepped up to the door and clicked the brass knocker, which was in the shape of an octopus. It reminded him of his best friend, and his heart lurched. *We'll find you soon, Sketchy! Just hang on!* he thought to himself.

X.

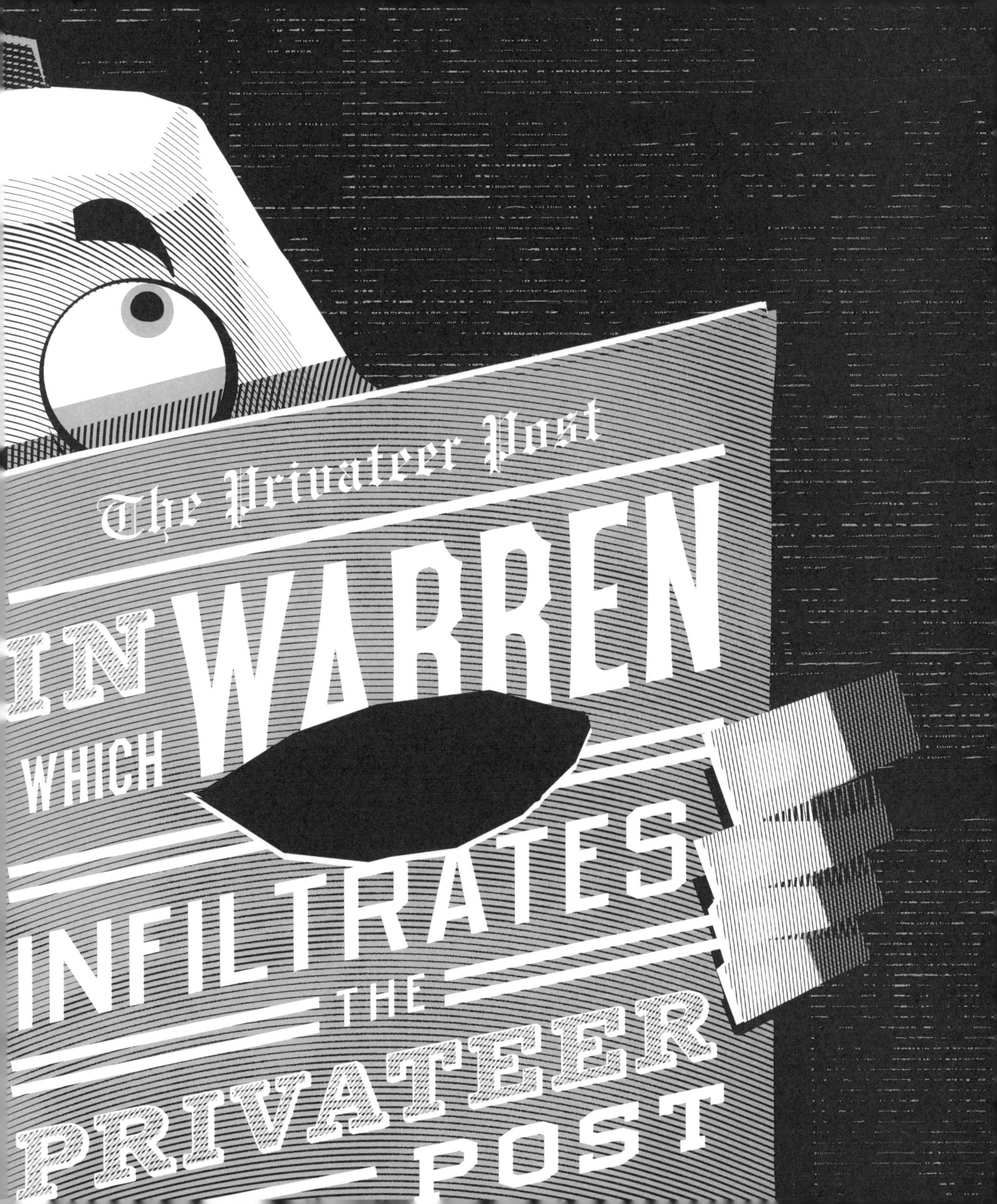
The Privateer Post
IN WHICH WARREN INFILTRATES THE PRIVATEER POST

The door swung open and a tight-lipped woman with her gray hair in a bun peered down at Warren through pointy spectacles. "We aren't interested in whatever you're selling!" she snapped.

"Actually, we're not selling anything. We're looking to buy," Warren said.

"Buy what?"

"Your most current newspaper. Tomorrow's edition, if you have it ready."

"We don't sell newspapers here; we make them!" the woman sniffed. "If you want a paper, find a shop that sells them."

She tried to slam the door in Warren's face, but Mr. Vanderbelly quickly stepped forward and blocked it with his arm. "Ahem! Allow me to introduce myself, madam. I am Mr. Vanderbelly, an esteemed journalist from Fauntleroy, and I—"

the woman said, and this time she slammed the door for good.

"How dare she!" Mr. Vanderbelly said. "It's almost as though the people of this wretched city have no respect for journalists!"

"THAT'S SCURVYVILLE FOR YA,"

Bonny snickered.

But Mr. Vanderbelly was undeterred. "We simply must get inside. I must see how their press operates!"

"They're not going to let us in," Warren said. "Let's just go find a shop that sells the paper. Which is what we should have done to begin with."

"Are you giving up so easily?" Mr. Vanderbelly said accusingly. "A true journalist never abandons a task. Not when there is a story to be told." And with that, he whipped out his notebook and began drafting a new article: "Infiltrating the mysterious *Privateer Post.* What are they trying to hide? Only I, Mr. Vanderbelly, can find out!"

"I could make a portal," Petula said, grinning mischievously.

"I thought you couldn't draw portals to places you've never been," Warren said.

"I can't draw portals to places I've never seen," Petula corrected. "But while that horrid lady was talking, I looked behind her into the building. I can get us inside."

"That would be trespassing," Warren said.

"Sketchy is worth breaking a rule or two for, don't you think?" Petula said. "We'll just slip in and out. Grab a newspaper and go."

"That would be stealing!"

"Leave a coin behind, if you must," Petula said. "We've already wasted enough time."

"He's too much of a chicken," Bonny said.

"BOK BOK BOK!" her parrot shrieked.

Warren sighed. "I'm not a chicken, I just—never mind. Fine, let's do it."

Petula drew a circle in the air, and a portal appeared. She stuck her head into it, then pulled back out. "O.K., the coast is clear! Bonny and I will wait here—it's easier to hide two people than four."

Warren stepped through the portal, feeling his stomach swirl like the inside of a washtub, and came out the other side. When his vision stopped spinning, he saw that he was in a large, dreary lobby. A desk sat nearby, no doubt the station of the unpleasant woman who had answered the door. Thankfully, she was nowhere to be seen.

"OOF! THIS IS UNPLEASANT!"

Mr. Vanderbelly gasped, straining to get through the portal. He finally managed to wriggle free and landed with a thump upon the floor.

Warren grabbed his sleeve and they hurried across the room, then through a doorway into the printing press area. Thankfully, the din of machinery covered up their footfalls.

The printing press was an impressive hulk of metal and gears. Steam hissed and pistons pumped and metal stamped as paper was rolled onto rattling conveyor belts to be inked with the day's news. Pirate workers dressed in dirty overalls tended the machine, yelling at one another as they fed paper into the proper slots. There was so much commotion, no one even noticed Warren and Mr. Vanderbelly enter.

They slunk along the edge of the room, hiding behind pipes and concrete pillars as they followed the progress of the machine from blank paper to printed page. Mr. Vanderbelly looked as giddy as a schoolboy. He scribbled furiously as he walked, attempting to describe every detail.

Finally, they reached the end of the machine, still unseen by the workers, whose arms were stained black with ink as they pulled fresh papers off the conveyor belt and tossed them onto a large stack. A young pirate paperboy stood nearby, dividing them into smaller stacks, which he wrapped with twine in preparation for shipment.

How could Warren grab one without anyone noticing?

"Incredible," Mr. Vanderbelly said in a low voice. "This machine puts the Fauntleroy press to shame! Look how quickly it runs, how smoothly. Pirate steam technology at its best. I must get a closer look—I must see its inner workings!"

"It's too risky," Warren said.

"Not for I!" Mr. Vanderbelly declared. "I am a journalist! I have immunity! Enough of this sneaking around."

Warren ducked behind a barrel as Mr. Vanderbelly stepped forward, revealing himself.

"Good day to all!" he said, gesturing grandly.

The workers started in surprise and the machine ground to a halt with a screeching of metal and a hiss of steam.

"My name is Mr. Vanderbelly, and I am an esteemed journalist from Fauntleroy! I could not help but admire your most impressive printing press, and I was hoping to write an article about it. Which of you will do me the honor of an interview?"

The supervisor, a tall, lanky pirate with a stubbly head, stepped forward, holding a large wrench in a rather threatening manner. "You're trespassin'! How'd you get in here?"

"Through a portal, if you must know," Vanderbelly said. "But enough about that—how is it that your machine is able to print so quickly? I would love to see its inner workings, if I might."

"He's come here to spy on us, Boss!" shouted one of the workers. "'He's here to steal our secrets!"

"Is that so?" The supervisor slapped the wrench in the palm of his hand. *PAT. PAT. PAT.*

"No, indeed!" Mr. Vanderbelly replied. "I merely came to learn!"

"SEIZE HIM!"

snarled the supervisor, and the workers descended upon Mr. Vanderbelly like a pack of wolves.

"I have immunity!" he cried. "Don't you know the journalists' code?"

"We pirates have our own code!" the supervisor barked as his workers tied Mr. Vanderbelly with the paperboy's twine and heaved him over their heads. "You want to see how the inside of our machine works? We'll show you!"

Warren watched in horror as they dropped Mr. Vanderbelly onto the conveyor belt and started up the press. The gears chugged to life with the sound of grinding metal. He had to do something—and fast—or else Mr. Vanderbelly would be pressed like a pancake!

"NOOOOO!" Mr. Vanderbelly shrieked as the conveyor belt pulled him closer and closer to the mouth of the press.

Warren saw a red emergency switch near the supervisor. Without another thought, he dashed forward, hoping to reach it before the priates realized what was happening. But he slipped in a puddle of ink and wiped out across the floor.

"Another one!" the supervisor cried. "Grab him!"

The workers leaped into action and tried to seize Warren, but the oily ink had coated his skin, making him as slippery as an eel. He wriggled out of their grasp and dashed for the emergency switch.

"HEELLLP!" Mr. Vanderbelly cried as his feet drew ever closer to a large metal stamper dropping onto the conveyor belt violently. *CLANG! CLANG! CLANG!*

The supervisor swung his wrench at Warren, missing him by a fraction of an inch. Warren tried again to yank on the switch, but his hands were too slippery. The supervisor swung again, and Warren ducked out of the way. The wrench swooped over his head and banged against the switch, sending sparks flying.

"No!" the supervisor cried when he realized what he had done. In his carelessness, he had smashed the emergency switch, causing the machine to screech to a halt. Warren used the distraction to rush over and pull his guest off the conveyor belt.

"Oh! What horrors!" Mr. Vanderbelly gasped as he shook himself free. "Let us flee this place immediately!"

"Don't let them get away!" the supervisor yelled, and the workers dashed after Warren and Mr. Vanderbelly as they made a break for the exit—but not before Warren snatched a copy of the paper from the freshly printed stack.

"Hey!" the pirate paperboy protested. Warren flicked the doubloon at him—the one the rooftop crows had gifted him—and the boy caught it in his grubby hands. He gaped at it in awe—it was worth 100 papers alone!

With the pirates hot on their heels, Warren and Mr. Vanderbelly plowed through the lobby and out the front door, spilling into the street where Petula and Bonny waited. Thankfully, Petula had a new portal ready and waiting, and Mr. Vanderbelly dove through it—only getting partially stuck before he managed to disappear all the way inside.

The pirate workers behind them skidded to a halt, fearful of the magical whirlpool.

"Arrgh! What's that?" cried the supervisor, taking a step back.

"Witchcraft!" the secretary cried as she burst out of the building. "Stay away from that thing!"

"Hurry!" Petula cried. Bonny jumped into the portal next, and Warren dove in after her. Petula leaped in last, closing it behind her.

The group landed with a thud on the wooden dock outside the hotel.

"At least I got the paper!" Warren said. He grinned weakly.

"Ooh, let's see," Bonny said, taking it from him. "Yep, this is tomorrow's edition. It's as current as it gets."

There came a sudden gust of wind, and the *Privateer Post* slipped from Bonny's fingers.

"Whoops!" she cried.

"BAD LUCK!" her parrot screamed.

"No!" Warren cried as the paper fluttered off the dock and cartwheeled over the water. After all that effort—everything was about to be ruined!

Without a second thought, Warren ran full speed to the end of the dock and jumped off, snatching the paper midair. He crumpled it into a ball and tossed it back to Petula seconds before splashing into the frigid water. It was unpleasant, but at least the ink from the press was washed away in the process.

"That was a close one," Petula muttered, shooting Bonny a stony glare.

Bonny scowled back.

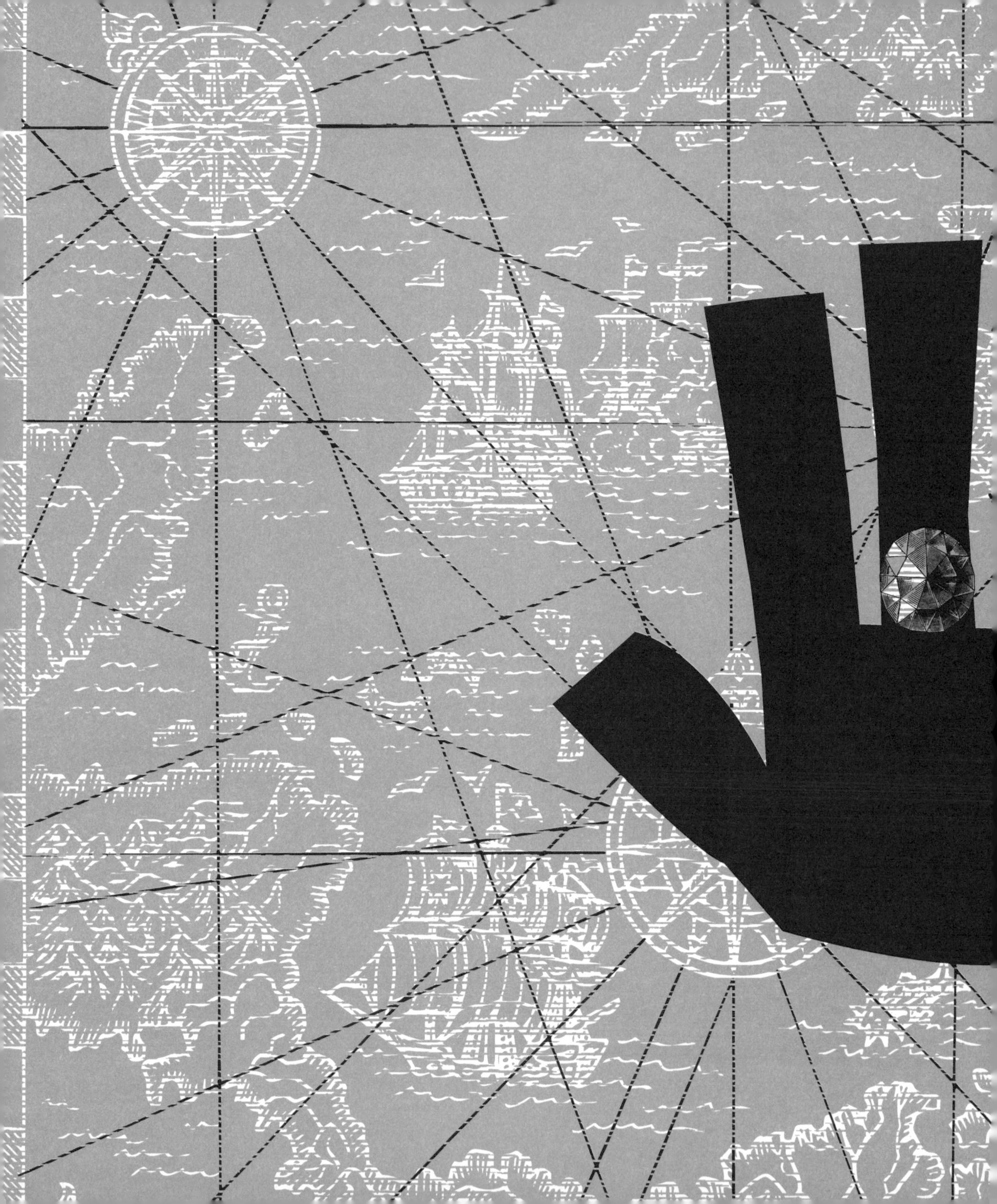

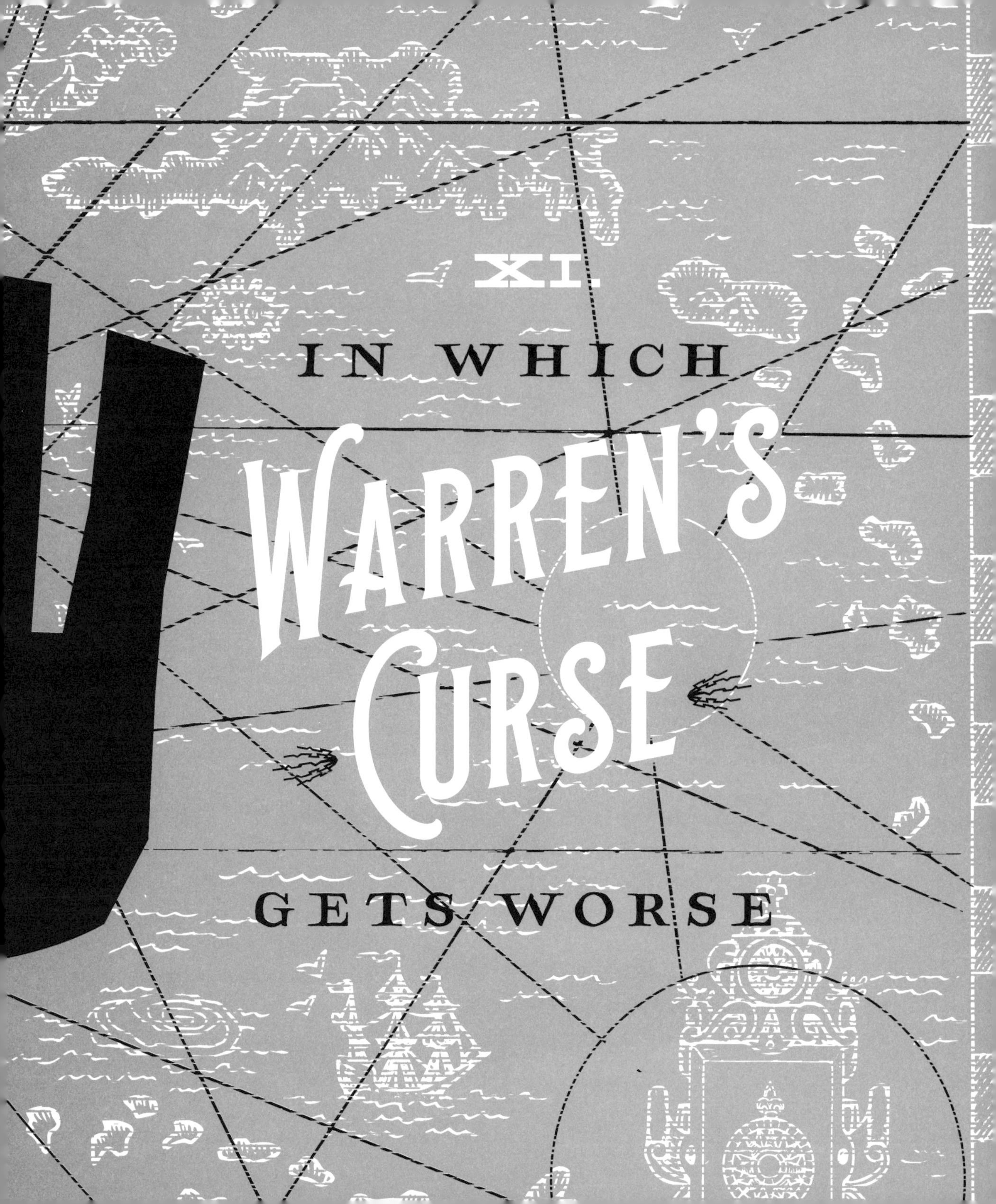

XI.

IN WHICH WARREN'S CURSE GETS WORSE

Warren wasted no time in steering the hotel away from Scurvyville. "Was there any trouble while I was away?" he asked Captain Grayishwhitishbeard.

"Yarr, just a little. But yer Beatrice put a quick stop to it. Pirates don't much like magic, you see. If there's one thing they're scared of, it's witches."

Warren smiled. He would have to thank Beatrice later.

As soon as Scurvyville was nothing more than a smog-colored smear on the horizon, Warren permitted himself to uncrumple the newspaper and read the latest puzzle from the sea circus. It was a riddle.

WHERE IS THE

SEA CIRCUS?

!!!

I live in the ocean
Though I do not swim

I stand on four legs
Though I do not walk

I drink from the earth
Though I have no mouth

What I do is messy
Though extremely refined

!!

Warren scratched his head in confusion.

"I wonder if there's a strange island somewhere," he said. "Maybe the legs aren't really legs, but towers of rock."

"Arr, in my travels, I've never seen a place like that," Captain Grayishwhitish-beard said, stroking his beard.

"Anyway, islands don't drink, either," Warren sighed.

"Maybe it's a trash island," Petula said. "Because it's messy."

"But how is that refined?" Warren asked.

"I guess it's not," she admitted. "And that still doesn't explain the drinking part."

"The riddle seems to be describing a living creature more than a place," said Warren.

"Maybe it's a giant turtle?" Petula suggested.

"What kind of turtle is big enough to hold an entire circus on its back?" Warren countered.

"Mmm, turtle soup," muttered Uncle Rupert from his hammock.

Warren and Petula made a face at each other. *Yuck!*

"So rich and oily . . . " Rupert smacked his lips. Then he frowned. "No, Mother, I will not wash my hands!"

"Does your uncle Rupert only dream about food?" Petula wondered aloud.

"Yes—oh! Wait a minute," Warren said, the gears in his head turning. "Rich and oily, rich and oily . . . "

He clapped his hands excitedly. "That's it! An oil rig! That's the next location!"

"I don't get it," Petula said, frowning. "What's an oil rig?"

"It's a special structure that sucks up crude oil from beneath the sea so it can be turned into diesel fuel to power things like automobiles," Warren explained. "The process of turning crude oil into fuel is called refining."

"I've never heard of such a thing," Petula said. "How do you know about it?"

"I learned about it from *Jacques Rustyboots and the Gas-Powered Galleon*," Warren said. "In the book, the hero stumbles across an oil rig and uses the diesel to upgrade his ship's engine, winning the annual pirate ship race."

"It's a good thing you read," Petula said, "otherwise this riddle would have had us stumped."

"Uncle Rupert solved it for me," Warren said. "Maybe he's smarter when he's sleeping."

"Pants sure are funny," Rupert giggled.

"Or maybe not," Petula said.

"Captain Grayishwhitishbeard, do you know of any oil rigs out here?" Warren asked.

"Arr, I do, indeed! There be a big one off the coast of the Crumbly Isles. It should be northeast o' here, but I'd double-check with yer navigator to be sure."

"I'll go tell Mr. Friggs!" Warren said, hurrying off to the library.

Bursting into the room, Warren could see that, despite his recent organizing, the library was already slipping back into disarray. He almost tripped over a stack of books placed randomly in the doorway, and for some reason all of Mr. Friggs's ceremonial masks were scattered on the ground instead of on the wall where Warren had hung them.

Warren slapped the newspaper onto his tutor's [still relatively tidy] desk.

"I solved the puzzle!" Warren announced. "We need to chart a course for the oil rig near the Crumbly Isles as quickly as possible. Captain Grayishwhitishbeard thinks it should be northeast of our location."

"I'm afraid we'll have to wait for dark and use the stars to navigate," Mr. Friggs said. "The compass hasn't been working properly."

He reached into a drawer and pulled out a large object the size of a dinner plate.

The compass's needle swung wildly, then reversed. Back and forth it went, as though searching for true north but incapable of pinning it down.

"What's wrong with it?" Warren asked in alarm.

"I wish I knew," Mr. Friggs said. "And I'll have to do my best without my tools—they're still missing. At least I still have my trusty map."

He reached for a rolled-up tube of yellowed paper and spread it across his desk.

"Oh, no!" he and Warren cried in unison. The map was covered in blotches of ink that blotted out most of the surface.

"It's ruined!" Mr. Friggs gasped.

"How could this have happened?" Warren said. "I know how careful you are with your maps!"

"I—I must have spilled a bottle of ink without realizing. Oh dear, this does complicate things."

"Maybe there's another map in the hotel.

This can't be the only one," Warren said.

"You're right. Check the game room. I do believe there could be a map in one of the bookcases there."

Warren hurried off at once, fretting over what bad luck he was having. It seemed like every effort he made to find Sketchy was being thwarted. Missing tools, broken compasses, spoiled maps.

It's the thirteen-year curse! he thought in despair. *Just when I think things are going my way, something bad happens!*

As Warren entered the game room, he could hear the clack of wooden balls being hit with a cue as a group of elderly pirates played a game of snooker. Five more sat at a table nearby, playing cards, and Sharky was with yet another group at the far end of the room; huddled together, they pored over some sort of jigsaw puzzle.

Warren went to the bookshelf, which was stacked with novels and strategy guides for winning at chess, checkers, and other games. He pawed through the books, but there were no atlases or maps that he could see. He sighed wearily.

"Whatsh wrong, lad?" the toothless pirate asked. "Me eyeshight may be poor, but even I can shee yer upshet."

"I'm just frustrated," Warren said. "It seems that everything I do, I—"An argument erupted at the other end of the room, cutting him off.

Warren went over to see what the commotion was. As he got closer, he saw that it wasn't a puzzle the pirates were working on . . .

"A MAP!"

HE CRIED HAPPILY.

And it was a splendid map, fully colored and with renderings of each island and continent on the globe. He could see that several large pins were stuck into the surface, marking various locations.

Two of the pirates were wrestling over a pin with a yellow head.

"Hand it over!" one growled.

"No, YOU!" the other snapped.

"Hold on!" Warren said. "Someone's going to get hurt!"

He gently pried the pin from their hands and held it securely. "What's this fight about?"

"Arr, each time we solve the riddle of where the Sea Circus will be, we stick a pin in the map marking its location," Sharky explained. "These louts are fighting over who'll get to do the honors. We take turns, ya see."

"She did it last time!" one pirate complained. "It be my turn!"

"But he does a poor job!" the other replied. "His hands are shaky and he always sticks it in the wrong place!

"All right," Warren said. "No more fighting in my hotel. Let's all go back to being friends."

He placed the pin on the coastline of the

"There! That's the next place the Sea Circus will be."

The pirates forgot their squabble as they leaned forward to inspect the locatioin.

"Now, do you mind if I borrow this map for a bit?" Warren asked. "We'll need it to get to where we're going."

"Go on ahead, Cap'n!" Sharky said. "Just bring it back in one piece! We've been tracking that Sea Circus for years."

"Aye, aye!" Warren said, and he hurried off to deliver the map to Mr. Friggs.

As he scurried up the stairs to the fourth floor, Petula burst out from around the corner, almost running into him.

"Waaah!" Warren cried.

Petula reached out and grabbed his lapels, preventing him from toppling backward.

"You must stop startling me like that!" Warren said when he recovered from the shock.

"Sorry. But listen, Warren, I'm very concerned." Petula glanced about, making sure no one was within earshot.

"What's wrong?"

"Everything!" she cried. "Haven't you noticed how things keep going awry? Items are going missing. Machinery is getting broken. There was a leak in the hull this morning that my mother and I had to patch up with magic!"

"Well, yes," Warren admitted. "But we have a hotel full of guests again. Things always get a little hectic when people are about."

"No, it's more than that . . . " Petula said, dropping her voice low.

Warren swallowed nervously and nodded.

"What? No!" Petula cried. "That's nonsense. What I mean is . . . Bonny!"

"Bonny?"

"She's behind all of this, I'm convinced of it!"

Warren digested this information, and then he shook his head. "No, I don't see how she could be responsible. She's been trying to help us."

"Is that what you call it? Warren, you're too trusting!"

Warren was growing a little cross. "I know you don't like Bonny, and yes, she's a little rough around the edges. But she's not used to having friends. She makes some mistakes, but she really does try."

Petula sighed. "Warren, I was in the dining hall this morning, and when Bonny walked by the table, all the silverware quivered. I think she had a magnet in her pocket!"

"So?" Warren said.

"So?! That's highly unusual . . . and suspicious!"

Warren couldn't help but think of the broken compass. Could Bonny's magnet have something to do with its malfunction? But why would she deliberately sabotage their progress? He decided he would have a chat with her later, but for now he had more pressing matters to attend to.

"I need to see Mr. Friggs," Warren said to Petula, a little gruffly. He didn't like what she was suggesting . . . but what if she was right?

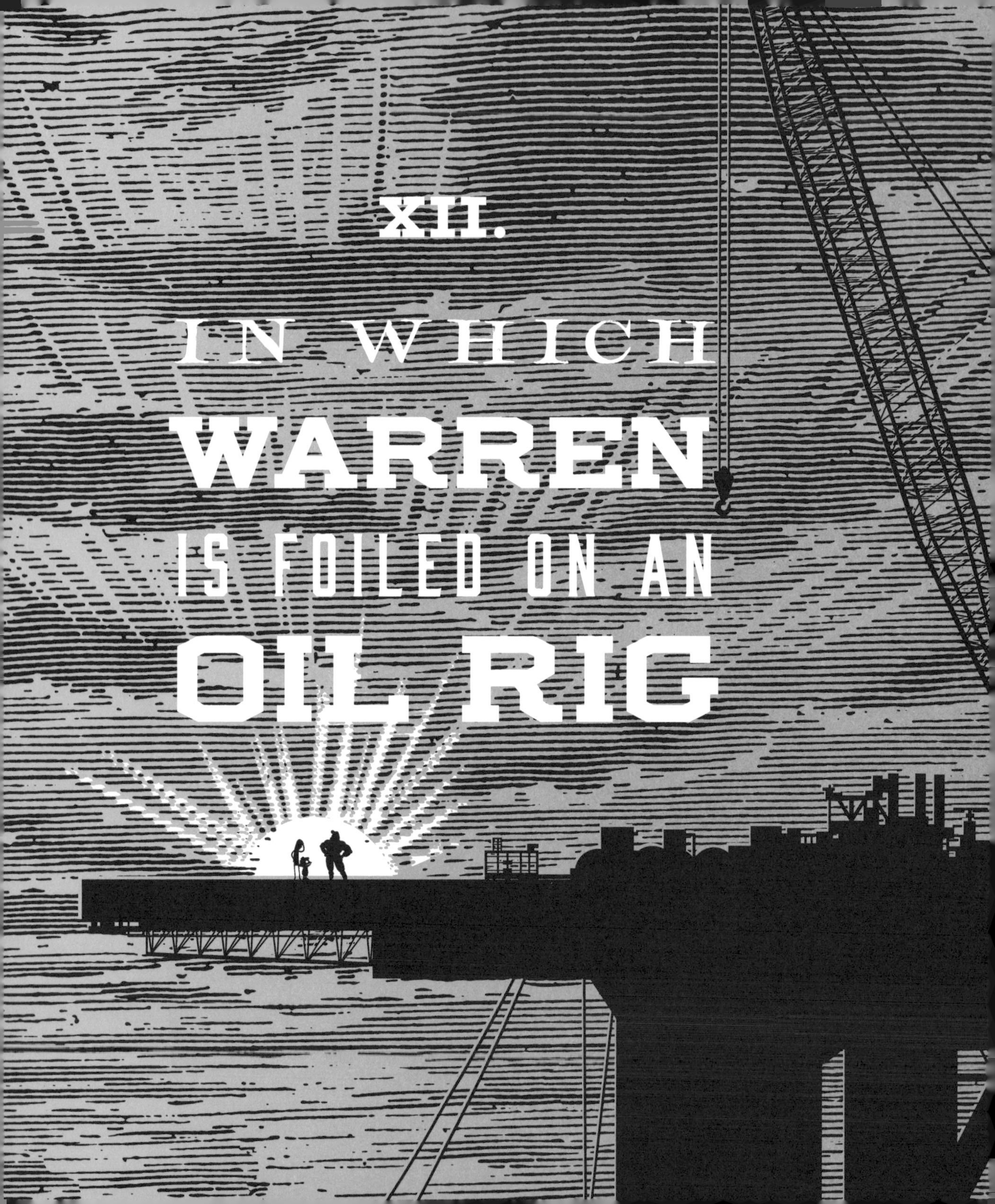
XII.
IN WHICH
WARREN
IS FOILED ON AN
OIL RIG

hanks to the pirates' map, Mr. Friggs was able to chart a course for the oil rig. Without a working compass, however, Warren had to stay on the roof all night, keeping an eye on the stars to ensure the hotel stayed on course. A blustery wind blew from the west, threatening to push them off track; Warren used the intercom to contact the control room and give Captain Grayish-whitishbeard instructions to adjust coordinates each time they drifted.

Warren huddled in his blanket and was grateful for the deep sides of the crow's nest, which helped protect him from the biting wind. He was reading *Jacques Rustyboots and the Caterwauling Coconuts* by the light of a flickering lantern. So far, Warren's hero had to contend with a band of sea witches riding sharks, a cannon battle with a fleet of rogue banjo smugglers, and, worst of all, a nasty cold—all while trying to transport a shipment of screaming haunted coconuts to a wealthy and mysterious client. As riveting as the story was, Warren's eyes began to droop. It was getting late.

Just as he was nodding off, the rooftop trap door squeaked open, jolting him awake. Warren peered over the edge to the deck below.

He could see Bonny, without her parrot for once. [That was a relief. The bird could be annoying at times!] He watched as she paced around, rubbing her chin thoughtfully. What was she up to?

"Bonny?" Warren called. "What are you doing?"

Bonny let out a squeak and jumped. Then she glanced up at Warren and scowled. "It's not nice to sneak up on people!"

"I'm sorry—I didn't mean to. You seemed a little lost."

"I'm NOT lost. I just came up for some fresh air."

"It's awful windy. Why don't you join me in the crow's nest?" Warren offered. "I could use the company."

Bonny hesitated, but then nodded curtly and began to climb the pole. She hopped into the basket and looked about appraisingly.

"Not bad," she said.

"I made it myself," Warren said proudly.

"Hmph," was all Bonny said to that.

"Here, share my blanket," Warren said, offering her a corner.

Bonny looked at it stubbornly for a moment, then pulled it over her knees.

"Say, you must be tired," she said. "Why don't you let me take a shift? I can keep us on track."

Warren recalled Petula's suspicion and instantly felt guilty for almost believing her. Bonny was only trying to help.

"Thanks, but I'm wide awake now," Warren said. "I've been wanting to talk to you, though."

"About what?" Bonny asked warily.

"Well, um, I just want to get to know you better."

"Ain't nothin' much to know," Bonny said. "You stole my pirates, so here I am."

"I didn't steal them," Warren protested.

"I'm just joking," Bonny said with a snort. "You're so gullible."

Petula's voice echoed in Warren's mind: *You're too trusting.*

"I'm sorry," Warren said. "I've been a little worried of late. All sorts of strange things have been happening around the hotel, and it's beginning to feel like something is up against me."

He watched Bonny closely to see how her reaction. A smile crept onto her face and she said, "You mean, like a CURSE?"

"Er, well, sort of!"

"That's because you're unlucky thirteen," Bonny stated matter-of-factly. "And it's even worse because you're the thirteenth Warren. The curse is doubled!"

"Yep," she said. "I wouldn't want to be you. Good thing I've still got a couple years before I turn thirteen. I don't intend to fall victim to any curse. I'll do whatever it takes!"

"Do you think there's anything I can do to stop it?" Warren asked.

"Well, if I were you, I'd quit sailing all over the globe trying to chase down your friend. The more you travel under a curse, the more likely things are to go wrong."

"But I can't just abandon Sketchy!" Warren cried.

"Why don't you wait till you turn fourteen? Then the curse will be over. It'll be a lot easier for you, I promise."

"But that's a whole year . . . "

"Hey, I'm only trying to help," Bonny said. "And I'm telling you, if you keep going forward, only worse and worse things are gonna happen."

Warren considered Bonny's words. Then he said: "Haven't you ever cared about anyone enough that you would even risk a curse to help them?"

"No, and why should I?" Bonny said. "No one's ever cared about me that much, neither."

Hearing this made Warren incredibly sad.

"That can't be true," he said. "Your pirate crew cares about you."

"Ha, yeah right! They cared so much they were ready to abandon Calm Waves and leave me behind."

Warren noticed tears glinting in Bonny's eyes. He wished he could say that she was wrong, but he knew she spoke the truth, and that made him even sadder.

"What about your parents?

Bonny shrugged. "They're gone. I was mostly raised by my gramps, but he's always traveling. He cares more about his own goals than he does about me."

Warren placed his hand over Bonny's. "Well, I care about you," he said. "In this hotel, you're family. This is your home for as long as you want it to be."

Bonny blinked and then stood up. "I don't need you. I don't need anyone." Then she crawled out of the basket and slid down the pole.

Warren heaved a sigh. Petula had it all wrong. Bonny wasn't bad. She was just hurt, and that made her lash out sometimes. He wished he could help Petula understand.

⚓ ⚓ ⚓

As morning broke, the irregular shape of the oil rig could be seen against the pastel sky. It stood alone in the ocean, a gangly structure on four tall legs, its upper body made up of steel panels, walkways, cranes, and fences. A flame shot out the top of a tall pillar like a beacon.

"I don't see the sea circus," Warren said as he peered through his periscope in the control room. Was he mistaken about the riddle?

"Maybe we beat it here," Petula said. "We did get that paper hot off the presses."

"Good point," Warren said, feeling heartened.

Warren and Petula accompanied Captain Grayishwhitishbeard upstairs, passing through the lobby and out the front door. Warren could see workers on the oil rig scurrying about like tiny ants.

"Ahoy!" he called out. One of the workers lowered a ladder.

"You two go ahead," Captain said. "I'll keep watch from here."

Warren and Petula nodded and climbed the ladder, stepping onto a metal gangplank where they were met by a stout worker wearing bright yellow coveralls and thick rubber boots that reached to his thighs.

"Hello, kids," he said. "What brings you out to these parts? We don't receive many visitors on this rig."

"We're looking for the Sea Circus," Warren explained.

"Oh, indeed!" the worker exclaimed. At the mere mention of the circus, more workers flocked around excitedly.

"It was amazing!"

"I've never seen such feats of strength!"

"The trapeze artists were death defying!"

"I had so much cotton candy I threw up!"

"You mean, it already came?" Warren asked, his heart plummeting.

"Came and left!"

"Oh, it was so fun!"

"There was a bearded lady with a trained monkey!"

"And the Great Eight—it's real!"

"Wait!" Warren said. "What's this about the Great Eight?"

"A new act—the star of the show!" a female worker said. "It whistled like an angel. The melody was so haunting and sad. Not a dry eye in the house!"

"I always thought the Great Eight was some silly pirate myth," said another worker. "But it's real!"

"Where is the circus now?" Petula asked. "Did they say where they were headed?"

"No, but they did load up on an awful lot of fuel while they were here. It seems they were preparing for a long journey."

"We were too slow!" Warren cried. "If only we had working navigational tools!"

"Don't lose hope," Petula said. "It can't have gone far."

"Well?" Captain Grayishwhitishbeard said when Warren and Petula returned.

"We missed it," Warren said glumly. "The circus is already on to its next destination. Wherever that may be . . . "

Warren returned to the lobby. Many of the elderly pirates were assembled there, eager for good news, but their faces fell when they saw Warren's expression.

"Young Warren returned with a glum countenance that those assembled took as a dire sign," Mr. Vanderbelly narrated aloud as he scribbled in his notebook. "Another setback in our young hero's journey!"

"I told you," Bonny said to Warren. "You're cursed."

"Enough of that!" Petula snapped.

"She's right," Warren said. He twisted the ring on his finger. How was it supposed to help him in situations like this? Maybe Mr. Friggs was mistaken about its purpose.

"We need to find another paper for the next riddle," Petula said. "Does that mean we have to go back to Scurvyville?"

"Never!" cried Mr. Vanderbelly. "I refuse to set foot in that horrible place!"

Warren shuddered. He didn't want to go

back either, but what choice did they have? If only there was a way to predict where the circus would be before it was printed in the paper. If only there was some sort of pattern . . .

That gave Warren an idea.

He ran directly to the library and burst in without knocking, startling Mr. Friggs, whose dentures fell out in surprise.

"Sorry!" Warren said, scooping them up and handing them to his tutor. "I just thought of something!"

"Oh?" Mr. Friggs said, working the dentures back into his mouth.

"I was wondering if there might be a way to predict where the sea circus will go before it's printed in the paper. And that made me curious to see if there might be a pattern based on where it's been in the past. If there is, we can use it to figure out where the circus will end up next."

"A marvelous idea!" Mr. Friggs said, pulling out the pirate map dotted with pins. "How lucky for us that those old pirates marked all the past locations for us."

"Not only that, but they marked each pin with a number indicating the order that each place was visited," Warren said, grabbing a pencil. "It's as easy as connect-the-dots!"

Carefully, Warren drew a line from the first pin to the second. And then from the second to the third, and so on. When he reached the final pin marking the oil rig, he stepped back to see what the lines formed.

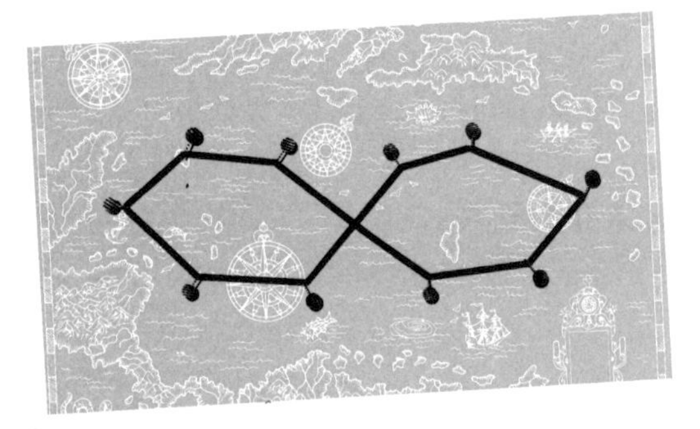

"There's definitely a pattern," Mr. Friggs mused.

"It looks like an infinity symbol," Warren said.

"So that means...the next location the sea circus will be...."

"Is in the center!" Warren exclaimed. "X marks the spot!"

Mr. Friggs clapped Warren on the back. "Brilliant, my boy! Simply brilliant!"

"But Mr. Friggs," Warren said. "I just noticed something . . . "

"What's that?"

"All the locations the circus has visited are islands or ports," Warren said. "The center one is in the middle of the ocean. Why would the sea circus go there if there's no audience to see it?"

Mr. Friggs's face fell. "You make a good point, I'm afraid."

"Perhaps we're mistaken," Warren said.

"It is easy to convince oneself to see a pattern where there is none," Mr. Friggs agreed. "What would you rather do? Take a chance on going to that point on the map, or go back to Scurvyville to find another paper?"

"They're in opposite directions," Warren said. "I don't know what to decide!"

"Well, how about I work on the coordinates for both," Mr. Friggs said gently. "In the meantime, you can think about which course to take."

Warren nodded and went to his attic room to think in peace. If he picked Scurvyville, they'd definitely find a hint where to find the next sea circus. But they might be too slow again. If he was wrong about the pattern, they would end up in the middle of the ocean, and even farther from his goal than before.

Perhaps it didn't matter what choice Warren made. As long as he was cursed, whichever path he took would be the wrong one.

"I need bad things to stop happening!" Warren cried in frustration. "And I need this ring to start working!"

He instantly felt a pang of guilt about feeling so ungrateful for his father's gift. Perhaps the ring was trying to help, though not in the way he expected it to. Perhaps "palimpsest" was an important clue.

Warren had been so occupied with finding Sketchy that he hadn't given much thought to the mysterious word. He unlatched the loupe on his ring and peered through it, looking around his room for invisible writing. Nothing appeared.

He pulled out his collection of Jacques Rustyboots novels and flipped through the pages as he peered through the loupe. Still nothing.

Suddenly, he had an idea. How did he not think of it sooner?

Warren reached under his pillow and retrieved his beloved journal, the one that had been written by Warren the 2nd, the builder of the hotel. It was all thanks to this book that Warren had learned the truth about the hotel's ability to walk. Perhaps it held more secrets.

He flipped to the first page and peered through the lens. Golden words appeared across the page, written in his father's hand. He was right!

Warren's eyes devoured the message:

My clever son,

If you are reading this, it means that you have found the journal I hid for you in the hedge maze, and that you have been given the ring to decode these words. It also means that I am no longer with you, or else I would have told you all of this myself. I'm sorry I made it so challenging, but I couldn't let this information fall into the wrong hands. I had to make sure that only you would be smart enough to solve the riddles I left for you to find.

You may have realized there is a curse upon this family. Many generations of Warrens have tried to break it, and all have failed, myself included.

But if anyone can do it, I believe you can!

You will be faced with many challenges, but the ring is the *key* to rising above them all. Use it wisely.

The hotel has been resting in a remote corner of Fauntleroy for so long, partly in an effort to hide from those who would do this family harm. The time for hiding is at an end. Surely by now you have figured out that the hotel can travel, but there are more secrets left to discover.

The only help I can offer is to share the advice my own father gave to me. He told me of a strange creature he had rescued from a horrible man many years ago. It was a tiny thing the size of his palm. It was shy and very afraid, and it slipped away down a hotel pipe, never to be seen again. My father told me to find this creature and to reunite it with the Great Eight. Unfortunately, I failed in this mission.

The Great Eight is the only thing that can break the curse.
If you can find the creature, it will help you.

Warren wiped away a tear. It was almost as if his father was in the room with him. He could hear his voice in his mind, as clear as a bell. Warren flipped frantically through the rest of the journal, but there was no more hidden writing to be found. Could the creature his father mentioned be Sketchy? His tentacled friend was far larger than a man's palm, but perhaps it had grown since his grandfather rescued it. After all, it had been lurking in the hotel boiler room for a long time before it chose to reveal itself to Warren.

He set the book down, his mind buzzing. So the Great Eight was real, after all—along with the curse. But how was he supposed to find the Great Eight, when so many others had failed? The Great Eight . . .

The Great Eight...

Warren bolted upright.

Thinking about the Great Eight had triggered a realization in Warren's mind—the pattern on the map wasn't an infinity symbol. It was an 8, turned on its side!

Warren didn't know what it all meant, but he rushed off to tell Mr. Friggs that he had made his decision.

Why hasn't the GREAT EIGHT shown itself?! I've been sailing in figure eights, as all the old legends instruct, and you've been whistling to call it from the depths . . . and still there's no sign of the monster!

It has been my dream—MY OBSESSION!—ever since I was a boy, to see the Great Eight with my own eyes and to receive its gifts. I've sailed in figure eights until I've gone dizzy, but it took me years to discover the piece I was missing.

YOU.

Tweeee?

That's right. And once I've fulfilled my dream, I can be done with this silly circus business once and for all.

Of course, that doesn't mean we can't give the audience a proper show in the meantime.

But understand this: if the **GREAT EIGHT** doesn't show up soon, there will be ... unpleasant consequences for you. So do not fail!

SLAM!

Tweeeeeee...

XIII.

IN WHICH THE WARREN

TO THE CHALLENGE

Warren sighed and pressed his head against the ship's wheel. "It's no use!" he cried. "The winds are blowing against us. We'll never catch the Sea Circus at this rate."

The hotel's progress was painfully slow as it navigated to the center of the infinity symbol on the map.

"I'm telling you, it's your curse," Bonny chimed in. "Besides, it's a terrible idea sailing to the middle of nowhere. What makes you think the sea circus will be there anyway?

"Just a hunch," Warren said.

"The whole point of a circus is to make money!" Bonny scoffed. "There's no customers in the middle of the ocean. If I were you, I'd go back to land and wait for your curse to pass. It'd be safer."

"Mmm, wafers," Uncle Rupert muttered in his sleep.

"I don't think this circus cares about making money," Warren said. "I think it's all a ruse."

Bonny's tanned face turned unusually pale. "What?"

"A ruse for what?" Petula asked.

"I believe they're really searching for the Great Eight," Warren said. "And that somehow Sketchy is involved. All the more reason to find Sketchy quickly."

Warren hadn't yet mentioned what he'd learned from his father's letter about the Great Eight and the curse. Until Sketchy was rescued, he could not afford to focus on anything else.

If only the hotel could go faster, Warren thought to himself. *It can walk. It can sail. If only it could fly.*

Wait . . . could it?

Warren looked at his ring. His father had said that it was the key to rising above his obstacles. What if he meant that literally? Warren rushed over to the controls and began running his hands over the panel, looking for anything that might be a keyhole.

"What is it, Warren?" Petula asked.

"The curse is making him cuckoo!" Bonny scoffed.

"CUCKOO!" her parrot mimicked.

"Are ye O.K., lad?" Captain Grayishwhitishbeard asked.

"I think my ring might be some sort of key," Warren said, and he continued searching the control panel for anything he might have missed.

But no—every button, knob, and latch was accounted for and had a purpose. He saw no hidden panels or triggers that might reveal another function of the hotel.

"Maybe I'm mistaken," Warren said, his excitement turning to despair. "Maybe it's nothing after all."

"Try the decoder," Petula suggested.

"Great idea," Warren agreed, and he flipped out the loupe. He peered through the lens and immediately noticed a glowing circle to the side of the wheel that wasn't visible to the naked eye.

"That's it!" he cried, startling everyone in the control room.

Even Rupert awoke with a start. "Danger?" he cried. "Where? Save me!!"

"It's fine, Uncle Rupert," Warren said, laughing. "There's no danger . . . unless you're afraid of heights."

"As a matter of fact, I am," he replied.

"Here we go!" Warren announced, and he pressed his ring against the glowing spot. A tiny round panel sank into the console, its seams so fine that it was impossible to see.

Lights flashed and the hotel's engine began to whir.

"Warren!" Petula cried, grinning, "you don't mean to tell me that—"

"This hotel can fly!" Warren finished. "Hang on tight, everyone!"

There was a loud clanking as an enormous hatch opened in the roof, revealing a giant balloon that was inflating with helium. Propellers jutted out from the hotel's sides, and with a *PUTT-PUTT-PUTT* they sputtered into motion. The entire structure vibrated as the engine keened even louder and the blurred propellers kicked into full speed.

With a lurch, the hotel began rising from the ocean. The cockpit window broke the surface of the water, giving them a bird's-eye

view as they shot into the sky. Water droplets streamed from the belly of the building as it soared upward, faster and faster.

"Woohoo!" Warren yelped as the hotel rose into the clouds.

"It's like being on a broom—but better!" Petula said. "I've never flown this high before!"

"Arr, and I've never seen the ocean from above!" marveled Captain Grayishwhitishbeard, looking out the window. "'Tis a beauty!"

"Hurrumph! Well, I don't like it," Bonny declared. "It ain't right to be in a flying building. It's unnatural!"

"I'LL SAY!" her parrot shrieked.

"I d-d-don't like it either!" Uncle Rupert stammered. Quaking, he clung to his hammock like it was a life preserver.

"Don't be scared, Uncle Rupert," Warren said. "Just pretend you're a bird!"

"He already is," Bonny said with a smirk. "He's a chicken!"

"WAAAAAH!" Rupert wailed. "That's not very nice! And now I'm hungry for chicken!"

Warren slowed their ascent and admired the ocean below as it glistened in the sunlight. From all the way up here, he could make out dark patches of coral, islands on the horizon, and the spray from a giant pod of whales in the distance. Captain Grayishwhitishbeard was right—it really was beautiful. He could see for miles in every direction.

Thanks, Dad, he thought.

Gently, Warren pushed the hotel forward. It glided through the air, skimming the clouds at a pleasant clip. After weeks spent bobbing on ocean waves, flying felt as smooth as glass.

Petula hugged him. "You figured it out, Warren! Now we'll find the Sea Circus in no time."

"Great," Bonny muttered.

XIII.

IN WHICH WARREN MEETS HIS IDOL

here it is!" Warren cried. He could make out the tiny shape of the sea circus at the exact location he had marked on the map—the dead center of what Warren had thought was an infinity symbol.

From above, it looked very strange—a colorful striped tent floating in the middle of the ocean. Warren could barely make out the floating platform it rested upon, or the two squat tugboats anchored beside it. There were also several pirate ships docked in the water nearby. Whether they were there as guests or for protection, Warren could not guess. But he wouldn't let anything stop him now.

"Sketchy, here we come!" Warren said as he eased the hotel downward.

Rupert pressed against the cockpit glass, forgetting his fear in the excitement. "Ooh, the circus! I can't wait! Can I have a hot dog and a tub of popcorn? Can I?"

"We're not here to have fun, Uncle Rupert," Warren said. "We're here to save Sketchy."

"Who?" Rupert asked.

Warren sighed. The hotel landed with a gentle splash, and Warren pressed the switch to lower the anchor. It was then that he noticed Bonny was scowling. "What's wrong?" he asked.

"I wouldn't get your hopes up," she said darkly. "Especially since you're cursed and all."

"We'll see about that!" Petula said. "Come on, Warren. Let's get out there."

Warren and his friends made their way to the hotel's front deck. Uncle Rupert clapped his hands like a little boy and shoved past everyone so that he was the first one out the door.

The circus tent loomed before them like an impressive beast. Warren had never seen anything so grandiose, with so many dazzling colors and patterns. He couldn't help but share a little of his uncle's boyish excitement.

Captain Grayishwhitishbeard laid down a wooden gangplank that linked the hotel deck to the sprawling platform the circus tent was staked upon.

"Me first!" Rupert cried, scrambling across the gangplank and barreling toward the tent.

Figures emerged from the tent flap that marked the entrance, and he stopped in his tracks. A tall man in a ringleader uniform strode onto the platform, flanked by a group of scary clowns who wore painted frowns instead of smiles.

"On second thought, someone else can go in first," Rupert said, backing away.

"Warren," Captain Grayishwhitishbeard said in a low voice, "I know that man."

But before Warren could ask who it was, the ringleader gave a sweeping bow and said, "Well, hello dear visitors! Welcome to the Most Amazingly Mysterious Sea Circus on Earth! Only the smartest and most clever can find my circus, so congratulations! You've arrived just in time for tonight's show."

"Your beard and gold teeth may be gone, but I'd recognize you anywhere!" Captain Grayishwhitishbeard snarled. "Jacques Rustyboots!"

The ringleader stood before his rival and smiled brightly. "Ah, Captain Grayishwhitishbeard, so we meet again!"

"WAIT—" Warren was stupefied.

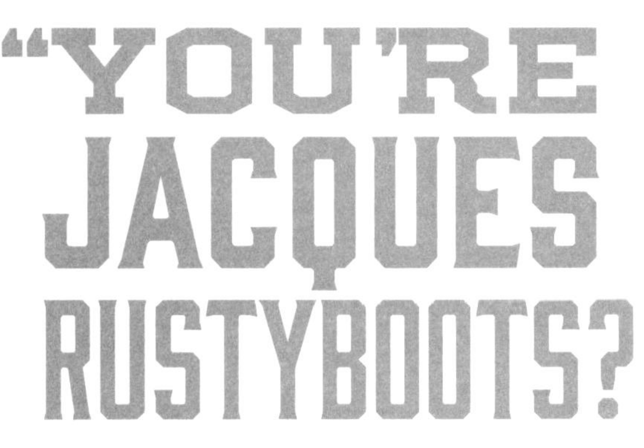

The Jacques Rustyboots?!"

"The one and only," the ringleader replied, bowing once more.

"I thought you were lost at sea!" Captain said.

"Not at all! Just lost in a different line of work," Jacques Rustyboots said with a chuckle. "Pirating simply wasn't lucrative enough, given the risks. I needed something more reliable to pay the bills while I continued my everlasting search for the Great Eight. And now, thanks to a recent acquisition, I'm closer than ever to my lifelong goal."

"You mean Sketchy," Warren said. His stomach lurched queasily. In all the excitement, he had momentarily forgotten that his hero was responsible for kidnapping his best friend.

"I hate to say this," Warren said, steeling himself, "but you're mistaken. You don't have the Great Eight. It's Sketchy. And it's a member of my family."

"Of course I know it's not the real Great Eight," the former pirate replied. "But my patrons don't know any better, and they're more than willing to pay the gold coins that fund my expeditions. Not only that, but this creature is going to help me lure the real monster out of hiding."

"Please, sir, Sketchy was kidnapped! We would really appreciate it if you'd let it come home."

"You're right about one thing," Rustyboots said, his face darkening. "The creature you call Sketchy was indeed kidnapped. But not from you. From me!"

"I—I don't understand," Warren stammered.

"I recognized that ring on your finger instantly," Rustyboots said with a sneer. "I knew your grandfather, Warren the 11th, and he stole my property! My most prized possession! He stole this Sketchy, and now I've finally gotten it back! So I will certainly NOT be handing it over."

"My grandfather wasn't a thief!" Warren blurted out.

"How little you know!" Rustyboots said. "And now history seems to repeat itself as you come here aiming to steal from me yet again. You little scoundrel!"

"*Some things never change!*" Bonny's parrot flew from her shoulder and landed on Rustyboots' epaulet.

"Ah, hello, McCrackers McCaw," Rustyboots said, scratching the bird under its beak.

Warren's mind was whirring with confusion. Why did Rustyboots call Bonny's parrot McCrackers McCaw?

His worst fears were confirmed when Rustyboots looked over at Bonny and said, "Well, Bonny. What excuse do you have for leaving behind the retirement home?"

"The pirates mutinied, Gramps! I had no choice but to go with them!"

"He's your grandfather?" Warren said in a hollow voice.

"It's all coming together now, isn't it?" Rustyboots said. "You weren't meant to find me, you know. Bonny was supposed to ensure that wouldn't happen."

"I tried, Grandpa! I sabotaged them! I hid their tools. I spilled ink on their maps. I used magnets to mess up their compasses. I did everything I could to stall them and stop them from getting here, but Warren is just too clever!" she said with a pout.

"I knew it!" Petula cried. "You were tricking us all along!"

"Betrayal!" Mr. Vanderbelly gasped, looking just a little too pleased about the news.

Warren's heart plummeted into his stomach. No one had ever turned against him like this.

"Bonny," he said, "I thought you were my friend." The young girl avoided his gaze, looking down at her boots instead.

"I told you, you were cursed," she mumbled.

"I'm disappointed, too, Bonny," Rustyboots said. "You failed me."

"Hey, you wouldn't even have the sea creature if I hadn't told you about it!" Bonny snapped. "You should be thanking me!"

"Ho, ho! That's my little spitfire!" Rustyboots crowed. "Very well, you have a point. Now come along. We have a show to prepare for!"

"Not so fast!" Warren cried, a fire rising in his belly. His pirate crew had streamed out of the hotel and gathered around him, fists clenched.

IN WHICH
The SEA

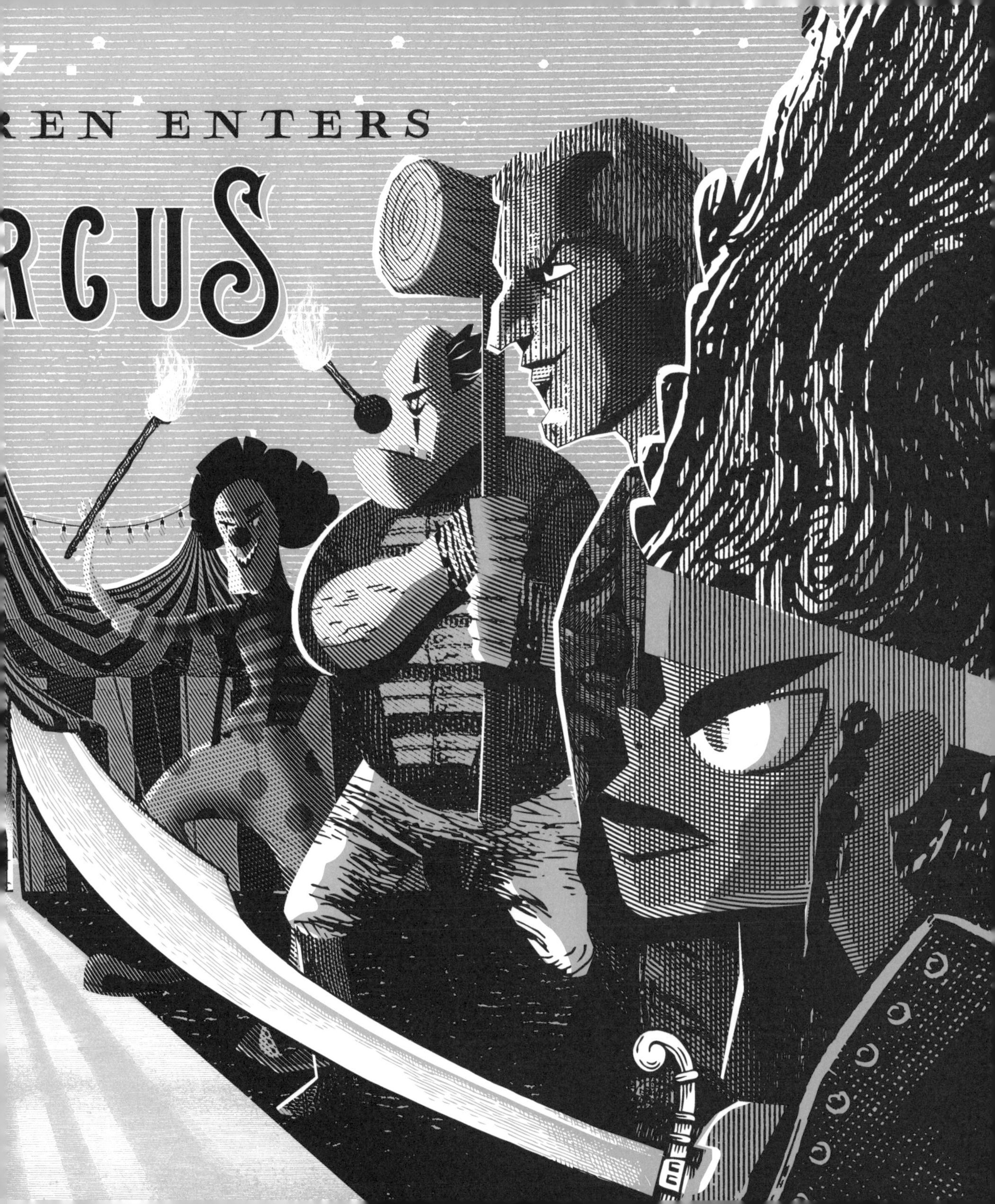
REN ENTERS
RCUS

Spoiling for a fight, eh?" Jacques Rustyboots said, baring his pearly-white grin. "You don't know what you're up against!"

"You don't know either!" Warren said. "I've got the finest crew in the world!"

There was a *THUMP!* as Beatrice landed on the platform from the hotel's crow's nest. Her eyes flashed angrily and she brandished her perfume bottles, one between each finger.

"Ha! You don't scare me, perfumier!" Jacques Rustyboots sneered. "I know those bottles can only trap witches! Enough of this nonsense. If you want to see your little Sketchy that badly, you'll have to earn it, fair and square."

"I'll do whatever it takes!" Warren said firmly.

Rustyboots turned and walked toward his tent. "Very well. Let's see if you can get into my tent unscathed." He paused and flicked his finger at his goons. "You know what to do." Then he disappeared and Bonny followed after him, giving Warren one last regretful look.

The clowns grinned wickedly and charged forward as the rest of their crew streamed out of the tent in a riot of clashing colors and patterns. Their shoes squeaked with each step. *HONK! HONK! HONK!*

"Waaaaahhh!" Rupert shrieked, running toward Warren in horror.

Fortunately, the pirates jumped into action with a battle cry, pulling out their rusty cutlasses.

"YAAAAAAARRR!"

"Fight 'em hard, crew!" Captain Grayishwhitishbeard roared. "Help Warren get inside that tent!"

Swinging a rubber mallet, a roly-poly clown charged at Warren, but Sharky dove between them and blocked the blow with his cutlass.

"Go on, lad!" he cried.

Warren began to run toward the tent, with Petula at his heels. She threw tiny fireballs at any clown who menaced them. It wasn't enough to do much damage, but it caused them to leap back, yelping from singed fingers and toes.

Amid the commotion, Warren ducked, twisted, and dashed this way and that, avoiding each new obstacle as it materialized: banana peels, flying bowling pins, firecrackers, paint-filled water balloons. To his delight, he saw Chef Bunion join the fray, using his juggling skills to toss clowns as though they were no bigger than mice. Beatrice was also leaping acrobatically to and fro, clearing a path for Warren and Petula. Even without her perfume bottles, she was a formidable opponent.

Finally, they reached the entrance to the tent and hurried inside. Outside, Captain Grayishwhitishbeard and the Calm Waves pirates continued to battle the clowns, and Warren was grateful for the distraction.

Panting from exertion, he and Petula looked around. They were in a small room with colorful striped walls and a creepy door painted to look like an open mouth lined with square teeth. A lone light bulb swung overhead, flickering with a sickly glow. Warren could hear the sound of distant cheering from deep within the tent. It seemed the show was starting.

"We better hurry," he said to Petula, grabbing the doorknob. But the door refused to budge. "It's locked!"

Just then, Chef Bunion entered the tent, followed by Beatrice and Mr. Vanderbelly.

"The pirates have the situation handled," he said, "so we thought you could use some help in here."

"As a matter of fact," Warren said, "any chance you can open this door?"

Chef Bunion rolled up his sleeves and yanked on the knob with all his strength. It still refused to budge.

"Stand back," he said, and then gave the door a mighty kick. It flew off its hinges, revealing a long tunnel painted with swirling stripes and glittery stars. It was spinning so fast, Warren was dizzy just looking at it.

"Come on," he said. "We have to get to Sketchy before the show starts!"

"Wait for meeeeeee!" cried Uncle Rupert, barging into the room. He was covered in paint and his clothes were tattered from firecrackers. He doubled over and took several heaving breaths. "I . . . hate . . . clowns!"

He looked up slowly and saw the spinning tunnel, his eyes widening with delight. "Oooh! Me first!" And with that Rupert ran into the tunnel, falling almost instantly.

"Tee-hee-hee!" he laughed, as his rotund

figure rolled around.

"Here goes nothing!" Warren said, and he stepped into the tunnel. Try as he might, he couldn't remain upright and toppled over at once. "WHOAAAA!"

Petula entered next and was instantly swept up and around.

Before long, everyone was being tumbled about in the spinning passageway, but only Rupert seemed to be enjoying himself.

"This is worse than going through one of your portals!" Warren said to Petula as they flailed their way to the opposite end.

At last, Warren managed to make it out, with Petula, Mr. Vanderbelly, and Chef Bunion all toppled on top of him in a giant pile. "OOF! OOF! OOF!"

Beatrice jumped out next, managing to avoid landing on the others, and she dusted off her knees daintily. Rupert, meanwhile, was still tumbling about, laughing hysterically.

"I feel like I'm in a washing machine!" he giggled.

"Come on!" Warren said, grabbing his uncle's arm and pulling him out of the tunnel. "We have to keep going!"

"You're no fun," Rupert pouted, but he looked a little green and wobbled unsteadily. The group continued on, passing through a doorway and into another room: a hall of mirrors. Some of the reflections made Warren look as squat as a bug, and some made him look as tall as a beanstalk.

"Who's that handsome fellow?" Rupert said, preening before a mirror that made him look far more muscular than he was.

"Stay together, everyone!" Warren said, inching his way forward. "It'll be easy to get confused in here!"

"Hey, where'd everyone go?" Rupert's voice called out.

Warren turned around. His uncle was nowhere to be seen, missing in just a matter of seconds!

Warren backtracked to find his uncle, but all the reflections bouncing back were confusing. Everywhere he turned he saw copies of Petula, Chef Bunion, Beatrice, and Mr. Vanderbelly . . . but no Uncle Rupert!

"Stay where you are, Uncle!" he called. "I'll find you!"

BONK! Warren turned a corner and ran smack into a mirror that made him look like a clown. He jumped back in horror. A clown-like Petula appeared beside him.

"I don't like this place, Warren!"

Somewhere in the distance, Warren could hear his uncle giggling. "Wheeeee! This is so fun!"

"Well, at least he's having fun," he muttered.

Beatrice pulled out a series of flashcards indicating a clock and an octopus.

"You're right, Beatrice. We're running out of time to save Sketchy," Warren agreed. "Let's keep going, and hopefully Uncle Rupert will stay out of trouble!"

The group inched along, groping their way around mirrored corners and across narrow corridors. It felt like the labyrinth would never end.

"The brave group was thwarted at every turn, confronted by their own fearsome visages! What horrors this chamber held—what trickery!" Mr. Vanderbelly narrated, doing his best to write in his notebook as he followed along.

Corridor after corridor they traveled, doubling back and getting more and more confused. Finally, they discovered a tall stairway made of mirrors. "Now we're getting somewhere!" Warren said. But when they climbed to the top, they were met with yet another corridor, this one leading to a dead end. Warren groaned in frustration.

"Maybe the exit is hidden," Chef Bunion suggested. "When I used to work in a circus, there were many hidden doors about."

"Good point, Chef," Warren said. He looked more carefully, noting how each mirror joined seamlessly with the next. Maybe there was a hinge somewhere that would indicate a doorway.

And then he felt something irregular beneath his shoe! Warren stepped aside and in the mirrored floor he saw the slightest crease where two mirrored tiles came together. A trap door!

He knelt down and felt around for a button or latch; the others stood around him expectantly. Not noticing anything obvious, Warren attempted to get his fingers around the tile and lift it up. That's when he heard a *CLICK* and all of a sudden, the floor dropped out beneath him!

"WHOAAAAA!" he cried as he slid down into the darkness.

"We're coming, Warren!" he heard Petula yell from above.

Warren landed in a giant pit of colorful balls—a soft landing, at least. The others plopped into the pit beside him, sending a spray of plastic balls bouncing across the room.

Warren crawled out and pulled out his friends one by one. Then they saw it: a door painted with the image of a large dagger.

"That looks ominous," Petula muttered.

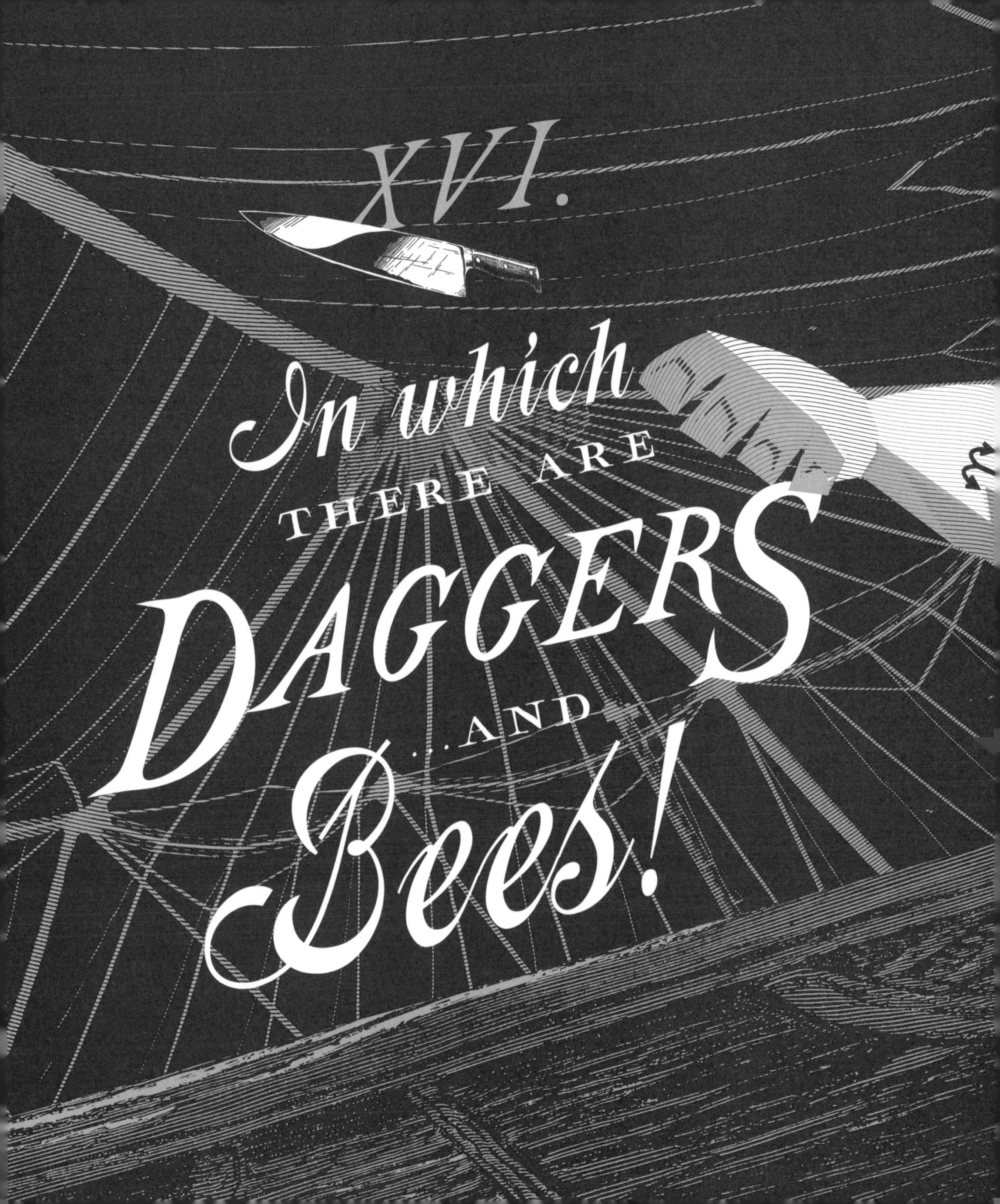

XVI. In which there are Daggers ...and Bees!

No sooner had Warren opened the door than a dagger whizzed by his face, embedding itself in the wall.

"You've been lucky so far," a clown said, twirling another dagger on the tip of his finger. "But now you have to get past me."

Beatrice dropped into a defensive stance, but the clown held up a hand. "There's no need for violence," he said. "If you pass my trial, I'll allow you to proceed."

"What do you want us to do?" Warren asked. The clown gestured toward a giant bull's-eye on the wall, scattered with black dots.

"This is a trial of precision. Hit the dots to proceed," he explained with a giggle. "It's quite simple, really."

"I'll do it!" Chef Bunion volunteered, stepping forward. "I've thrown daggers during my circus days, and in the kitchen, too. This will be a piece of cake!"

"Not so fast," the clown said. "We need a volunteer to strap themselves to the board."

Warren and Petula exchanged nervous glances.

"I would certainly volunteer," Mr. Vanderbelly said, "but it would prevent me from making an accurate record of this event. A journalist must remain impartial, you see."

Beatrice nodded curtly and stepped toward the bull's-eye.

"Mom, no!" Petula cried.

Her mother winked at her as she strapped herself to the board. *It's okay,* her smile said.

"Don't you worry, lass," Chef Bunion assured Petula as he accepted a handful of daggers from the clown. "I've got this."

"Ah, ah, ah!" the clown said, waving a finger. "You're forgetting the most important thing. A blindfold!"

The clown stepped forward and tied a thick cloth around Chef Bunion's eyes. Warren saw Chef swallow hard. Could he still do it?

"I can't look," Petula said, though her eyes remained glued on her mother.

Chef took a deep breath and hurled the first dagger. It cartwheeled through the air toward Beatrice's body. She remained passive and unblinking as it hit the wood—*THUNK!*—mere inches from her neck.

"Lucky shot," the clown said. "There's still five more."

THUNK! THUNK! THUNK! THUNK! In rapid succession, the daggers hit their marks spot-on! Warren wanted to let out a cheer, but he dared not make a noise, lest it distract Chef.

"Just one more!" Petula whispered,

clinging to Warren's arm.

"Hmph," the clown grunted. "This is too easy!" He stepped up to the bull's-eye and gave it a push. It began to spin like a wheel, and Beatrice along with it.

"That's not fair!" Petula cried. "How is he supposed to know where to aim?"

"Don't you worry," Chef said reassuringly. "I have more senses than sight alone!"

He licked his finger and tested the air, then sniffed a couple whiffs with his bulbous nose. Warren had no clue how this might help him land the dagger, but who was he to question Chef's ways?

WHOOSH! The final dagger flipped through the air in a blur and seemed as though it was headed right for Beatrice's face. *THUNK!* But Chef's timing was perfect—the dagger hit the mark just above her head.

"Impossible!" snarled the clown.

"Remarkable!" cried Mr. Vanderbelly.

The sound of machinery whirred to life when the dagger hit its final mark, and the bull's-eye swung away, revealing another passage.

"Let's move on!" Warren said, helping Petula undo Beatrice's straps.

"No! You can't proceed!" the clown cried, leaping in front of the doorway. "The ringleader will have my head!"

"We passed the test fair and square!" Chef Bunion said. "Get out of the way!"

"I won't let you pass!" The clown let out a sharp whistle, and in burst several acrobatic fire-dancers, twirling batons of flame.

Chef wrestled the clown away from the exit as Beatrice leaped forward to spar with the acrobats, flipping and dodging streaks of fire as she kicked the legs out from beneath them.

"Go on!" Chef yelled to Warren. "We'll hold them off!"

Warren nodded. He felt a little uneasy leaving his friends behind, but he knew they could handle anything. The sound of cheering grew louder as Warren, Petula, and Mr. Vanderbelly raced into the next room.

"Sounds like we're getting closer!" Petula said.

This new space appeared empty, save for a small stage at the far end.

"The coast is clear," Warren said. "Hurry!"

They ran across the room toward the exit, but just as they passed the stage, a spotlight flicked on and a loud voice proclaimed: "Step right up! Step right up! You're about to witness the most bizarre, the most grotesque, the most SHOCKING sideshow attraction you've ever seen!"

Despite themselves, Warren and the others stopped to stare as the curtain parted and a burly man in a lumberjack outfit stepped onto the stage. His golden beard caught the light strangely. In fact, it seemed to be moving.

Warren squinted. What the—?

"Bees!" he realized with horror.

"That's right!" the voice continued. "It's the infamous Man with the Beard of Bees! Formerly a lumberjack from the Malwoods, Mr. Bee Beard made the grave mistake of destroying a hive while chopping down a tree. He has since been doomed to use his own face as their nest—or risk their wrath!"

"It's been twenty years," said Mr. Bee Beard in a gravelly voice. "I can barely remember the look o' my own face. My wife screamed and turned me away. Even my own mother wouldn't take me in. So I roamed the forests and the mountains, hungry and lost, till I found my home in this here sideshow."

"That's awful," Warren said, feeling genuinely moved.

"One good thing about having a beard of bees is having a thousand friends at all times," the man continued. "I tell 'em my secrets. I teach 'em tricks."

"Well, that's nice?" Warren agreed.

"I trained my bees well. They respect me and follow my commands."

"T[illegible] good?" Warren said. "Anyhow, it was lovely meeting you, but we must be on our way. Good luck with your, uh, beard!"

Warren, Petula, and Mr. Vanderbelly moved on to the exit, only to find it locked with a padlock.

"Drat!" Warren cried. "Not another lock!"

"No worries! I can melt this with a fireball," Petula said. "It'll just take a minute."

A flame emerged from the tip of her finger and she set to work, engulfing the lock in a flame.

"I'm afraid my bees and I cannot allow that!" Mr. Bee Beard yelled from the stage. "SIC 'EM!"

There was a loud humming noise as the bees moved in a swarm away from the man's face.

"Oh, no!" Warren cried, hearing them buzzing angrily. He looked around for someplace to hide, but there was no refuge from the impending attack. Surely they'd be stung to death!

"Fear not!" Mr. Vanderbelly announced valiantly. "I once wrote an article all about bees, I know their weakness!"

"You what?" Warren exclaimed as Mr. Vanderbelly leaped into action. He tore several sheets of paper from his notebook, curled them into a cone, and waved them in front of Petula's flame until they caught fire.

"What are you doing?" Petula yelled.

"Just worry about that lock!" Mr. Vanderbelly said. "I'll hold off those pesky bees!"

Warren watched in astonishment as Mr. Vanderbelly waved the flaming paper cone in the air. Almost instantly, the cloud of bees faltered, appearing dazed as smoke from the fire wafted about them. They buzzed in confused circles, knocking into the walls and ceiling.

"My bees!" Mr. Bee Beard cried in horror. "What are you doing to them? Stop it!"

"Smoke," Mr. Vanderbelly explained. "It relaxes them."

THUNK! At last, the molten padlock fell to the floor. "It's open!" Petula announced.

"Come on!" Warren yelled. "Let's get out of here!"

"You go on ahead!" Mr. Vanderbelly said. "If I stop smoking the bees, they'll be twice as angry and chase us for miles!"

"Are you sure?" Warren said, shocked at Mr. Vanderbelly's sudden show of selflessness.

"I can handle it! Go on!"

"Thanks!" Warren said, and then he followed Petula out the door. This was a side of the journalist he hadn't seen until now, and he rather liked it.

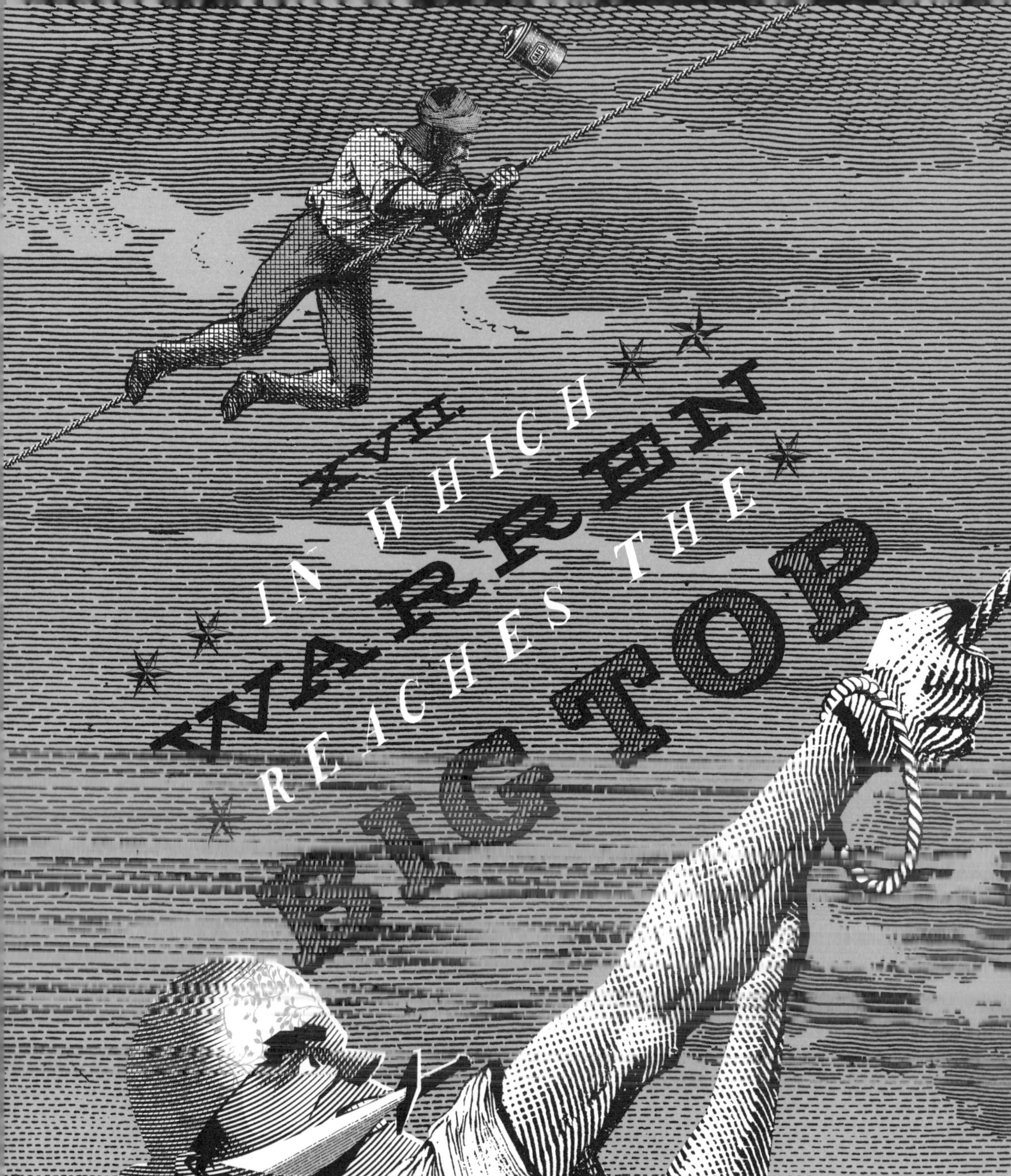
XVII
IN WHICH
WARREN
REACHES THE
BIG TOP

Warren and Petula emerged from the chaos and stepped into a new room. It was dimly lit and wavered with soothing blue light that reflected off a lazy, artificial river, which snaked its way from one end of the room to the other, disappearing into a tunnel twinkling with fairy lights. Overhead, a banner in curly script read: "Tunnel of Love." Upon the water was a series of vacant swan-shaped boats, slowly drifting along the current in a row. One by one, they disappeared into the tunnel as a sappy melody crackled over a speaker.

Warren and Petula said in unison.

"Looks like there's only one way forward," Petula said, gesturing toward one of the boats.

Warren hopped in, then helped Petula in after him. They both sighed wearily as the boat drifted toward the tunnel at a gentle pace. It felt good to rest their feet after so much activity. Within seconds, the love tunnel had engulfed them, and Warren could barely make out Petula sitting beside him, save for the barest outline provided by the dim illumination from the twinkle lights overhead. The music swelled into a sweeping crescendo, and Warren coughed nervously while Petula fidgeted. The boat was moving awfully slow, and Warren wondered how long the lazy river actually was.

"So," Warren said.

"So," Petula said back.

There was an awkward silence as Warren tried to think of something to say. Finally, he said, "I'm sorry."

"For what?" Petula asked.

"For not believing you about Bonny. I should have listened."

Petula sighed. "It's one of my favorite things about you—you always see the best in everyone. I'm just sorry Bonny let you down."

"Me, too. But I can't dwell on that now. What matters is bringing Sketchy home."

"Exactly," Petula said, squeezing his hand. "And we're getting close. I can feel it!"

Almost as if on cue, the tunnel brightened as they approached the exit. The romantic melody was smothered by blaring circus trumpets, drums, and the sound of boisterous cheers. The scent of buttery popcorn filled the air as the tunnel opened up into the big top. The enormous center ring was circled with stands, all packed with rowdy pirate spectators. Up above, a trio of acrobats were holding onto one another's ankles as they swung precariously on a trapeze. Spotlights swerved to and fro, illuminating them and making their sequined outfits sparkle. In the ring below, a strong man hefted an enormous barbell in one arm as roaring lions and tigers prowled around him. A lion tamer kept them at bay with a smart snap of her whip. As though that spectacle wasn't enough, a group of clowns were gathered on the sidelines, causing mischief and throwing pies at one another to make the audience laugh. Warren was so dazzled by all the sights, he almost forgot to exit the boat before it disappeared back into another tunnel.

Petula tugged on his sleeve and whispered: "Come on!"

Warren hopped out of the boat and looked around. Sketchy had to be nearby. A bearded lady emerged from a flap on one side of the tent and made her way toward the ring. A tiny monkey wearing a sport coat and a fez followed at her heels, playing a miniature accordion.

"There!" Warren pointed to the flap the woman had emerged from. "That must be the backstage area."

He and Petula crept toward the opening, trying to remain hidden. Each time a spotlight swept overheard they froze like rabbits, but thankfully no one seemed to notice them. There were simply too many other wondrous sights to see.

Just when they reached the flap, the lights in the tent dimmed and a drumroll began.

"LADIES & GENTLEMEN! BOYS AND GIRLS! PIRATES AND PIRATESSES!"

Rustyboots's voice rang out as he stepped into the center ring. "Tonight, for our most amazing and final act, I promise you a show the likes of which you have never before seen! For the first time ever, I present to you the most legendary, powerful, and elusive creature known to man. That's right!

The LEGENDARY GREAT EIGHT, MASTER OF THE SEAS, BESTOWER of GIFTS, CREATOR OF STORMS!"

The audience roared its approval. "We better hurry!" Warren whispered.

He yanked aside the tent flap an inch and peered through the gap to see if the coast was clear. On the other side was a small room filled with assorted circus props: barbells, Hula-Hoops, costume racks, and barrels of fireworks. A woman in a colorful leotard was seated at a vanity, putting the finishing touches on her makeup. Warren was wondering how they would get past her when suddenly she stood, adjusted her feather cap, and made her way toward the exit. Warren and Petula jumped back, covering themselves with the flap as the woman walked past. Warren and Petula let out a sigh of relief, then slipped into the room.

"Sketchy?" Warren said as loud as he dared.

He heard a weak whistle. "Tweee?"

"Sketchy!" he cried, and hurried toward the sound. He shoved aside a clothing rack, revealing a cage. Sketchy was slumped inside; it was wearing a frilly collar and its body was painted with garish makeup to make it look like a sad clown. Despite its morose appearance, Sketchy perked up at once upon seeing its friends. Its tentacles reached through the bars, embracing Warren and Petula as best it could.

"Oh, Sketchy!" Petula cried. "What have they done to you?"

"We're going to get you out of here!" Warren said, and he began examining the cage, looking for a latch. Heavy chains lashed around the bars, holding them tight.

"Hurry," Petula said, "I think Jacques Rustyboots is almost done giving his speech, which means it's Sketchy's time to go on stage."

"I can't open the cage!" Warren cried. "Petula, can you melt these chains with your fire magic?"

"It would take too long," Petula said. "Oh, I wish my portal was big enough to transport Sketchy back to the hotel!" she lamented. "If only my mom was here."

"Your magic is stronger than you think," Warren said. "And together we can figure this out."

He looked around and found what he was looking for: a sturdy rope. He tied it securely to the bars and handed Petula the other end.

"How's your rope magic?" he asked.

She smiled. "Stronger than I think?"

"Good answer!" Warren said. "Try to attach this rope to the hotel, and then tell Mr. Friggs to start the engine and take off."

Petula grinned. "I like where you're going with this! You got it, Captain!" She grabbed the end of the rope and closed her eyes in concentration. Within seconds, the rope began to jump and wiggle like a snake, and Petula held on tight as it lashed her to and fro. "Whoooooaaa!" she cried.

"You can do it, Petula!" Warren said. "Concentrate!"

Petula nodded and gritted her teeth. "Down, you pesky rope! Stay!" The rope jerked to a stop and seemed to stand at attention. Carefully, Petula released it and stepped back.

"Now, follow my command!" she said. "Lash yourself to the hotel outside, and do it fast!"

The rope seemed to nod and then shot forward, ripping a hole in the tent's fabric as it made a beeline for the hotel.

Petula drew a portal and hopped in. "I'll tell Mr. Friggs what to do!" she assured Warren, and then she disappeared into the mist. Warren felt a tug on his end of the rope as it lashed itself to the hotel.

"Get ready for liftoff," Warren said to Sketchy as he climbed to the top of the cage. He held on tight, anticipating a rough ride.

Suddenly, the flap flew open and Jacques Rustyboots stormed in. "You again!" he yelled in shock. "You weren't supposed to make it this far!"

"Surprise! I got past all your obstacles!" Warren said proudly. "And now I'm leaving with what I came for!"

Rustyboots snarled and stormed toward the cage. "I think not!"

"Anytime now, Petula," Warren whispered anxiously.

Rustyboots reached the cage and tried to grab ahold of Warren. Sketchy whistled sharply and used its tentacles to try to bat Rustyboots away, but it couldn't do much behind bars. Warren edged backward as Rustyboots's hand grazed his foot. The man's eyes flashed with rage, making him look more like a lunatic and less like the hero Warren knew from his beloved books.

"Get over here, you little—"

Suddenly, a sound rattled through the air—*RATATATATATATATATAT!* It was the hotel's propellers!

In an instant, the cage lifted off the ground, ripping through the ceiling and knocking aside the support beams. Jacques Rustyboots fell backward in shock as the tent collapsed around him, revealing the stunned audience seated within the big top. The spectators struggled amidst yards of torn fabric and gawped at the unusual sight of a giant hotel hovering overhead, its many propellers slicing the air with deafening noise.

"Get back here!" Rustyboots roared.

The hotel rose higher and higher, and with it Warren and Sketchy, the cage trailing by the end of the rope.

"Stop them!" Rustyboots cried, stumbling into the center ring. "Fifty thousand doubloons to the one who brings me that squid!"

The announcement of such a large sum immediately attracted the pirates' attention. The mob of them poured out of the stands and scurried toward their ships anchored nearby. They cheered lustily and waved their cutlasses, hungry for the promised reward.

Warren watched the commotion below, confident that he and Sketchy were safely out of reach . . .

WHOOSH! A harpoon tied to a rope sliced through the air, shot from a pirate ship below.

"Oh, no!" Warren cried, and Sketchy released a teakettle sound of alarm as cannons boomed. More and more harpoons whizzed past.

"Higher!" Warren yelled, even though he knew no one in the hotel could hear him.

THUNK! A harpoon landed on the side of the hotel, its barbed metal sinking into the wood. *THUNK! THUNK!* Two more hit home, and the hotel gave a jerk before stopping in its tracks.

Warren looked down and saw pirates scaling the ropes to the hotel, clenching daggers between their teeth.

"AAAARGH! Hold 'em off, crew!" commanded Captain Grayishwhitishbeard from above.

Warren looked up to see the Calm Waves pirates leaning out of windows as they threw books, silverware, pottery, furniture, and anything else they could get their hands on at the encroaching invaders. Several of the opposing pirates were knocked from their harpoon ropes and splashed into the sea. But for every pirate who was stopped, three more were climbing up. The assault was unrelenting. Warren wished he could do something to help.

He decided that he could at least call out some encouragement. "You're doing a great job!" he yelled. "I believe in every one of you!"

"Tweeeeeee!" Sketchy added helpfully.

"How sweet," came a voice from behind. Warren spun around to see Jacques Rustyboots hovering midair! Then he realized Rustyboots wasn't actually floating—he was being carried by parrots, including McCrackers McCaw.

"Tweeeeeeeee!" Sketchy trilled angrily. It tried to use its tentacles to bat Rustyboots away, but it was no use. The parrots deposited their leader on top of the cage and swooped off. Rustyboots pulled out his cutlass and began sawing at the rope that connected the cage to the hotel above.

"Nooooo!" Warren cried, trying to stop his pursuer. But he was just a thirteen-year-old boy, and Jacques Rustyboots was a tall and strapping former pirate. Warren's efforts were about as effective as a gnat's. The cage shuddered as the rope began to unravel. Rustyboots's face was a rictus of glee and fury as he continued to cut through the many layers of twine.

"Almost there!" he hissed.

Warren resorted to biting Rustyboots's arm. That seemed to have an effect.

"YOW! You little brat!" And with a powerful sweep of his arm, Rustyboots sent Warren tumbling off the cage.

"Aaahhhh!" Warren cried as he fell. Fortunately, Sketchy reached out a tentacle and caught him at the last second, pulling Warren up so he could grab the bottom of the cage. He then attempted to climb up the side, but his hands were sweaty and slipped on the bars.

The cage shuddered again. The rope was down to only a few strands.

"We're going to fall!"

Warren locked eyes with Sketchy, and he saw his own fear reflected in his friend's many eyes.

Sketchy began to whistle a tune. It was so sad and so lovely, just the sound of it made Warren want to laugh and cry all at the same time. Even Jacques Rustyboots stopped what he was doing and stared at Sketchy mournfully.

Suddenly the air around Warren seemed to vibrate, and his ears rang with pressure. A low rumble erupted from the ocean, and the water began to churn and froth.

"BRRRRREEEEEEEEEEE!"

Something was coming...

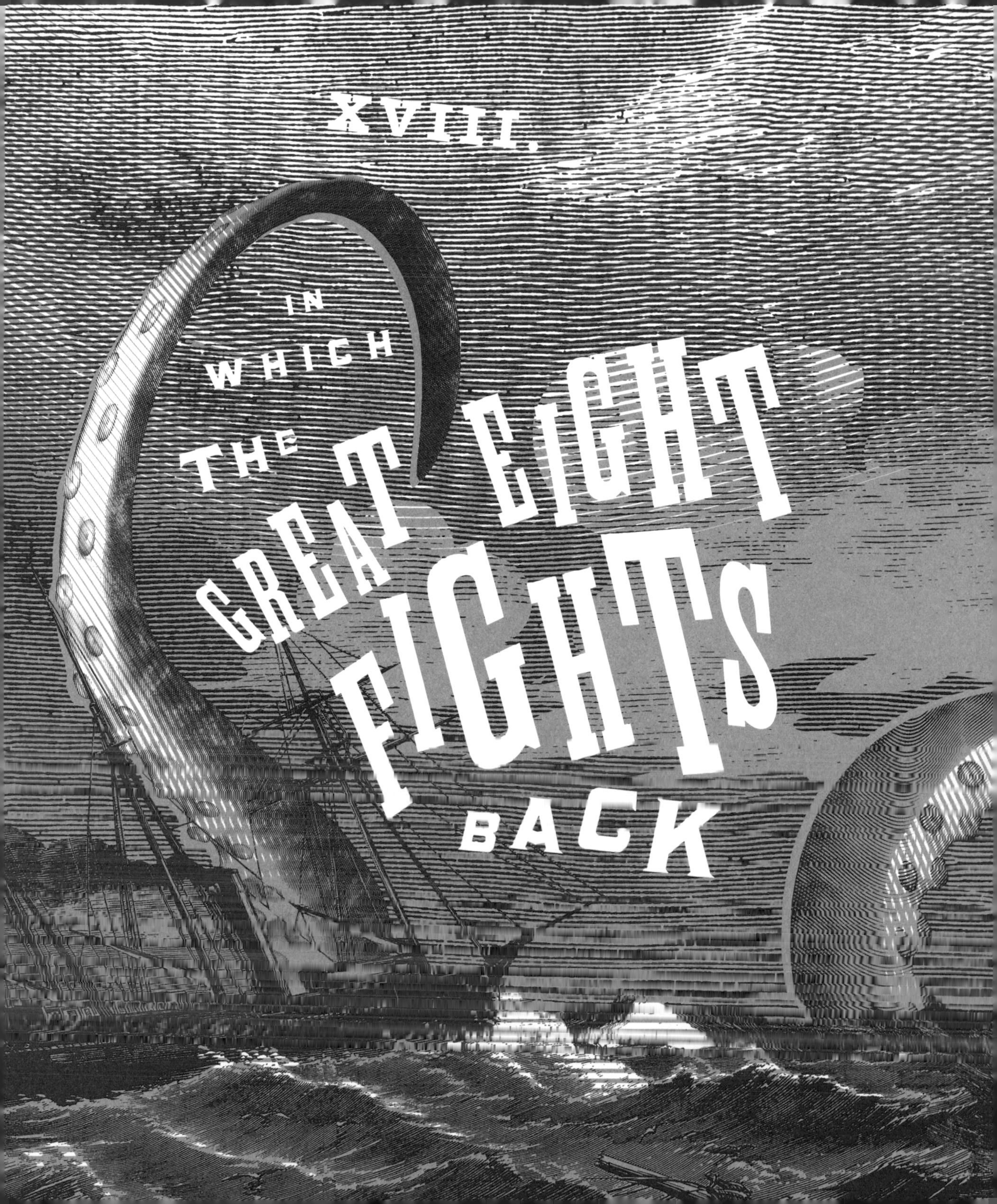
XVIII.
IN WHICH
THE
GREAT EIGHT
FIGHTS
BACK

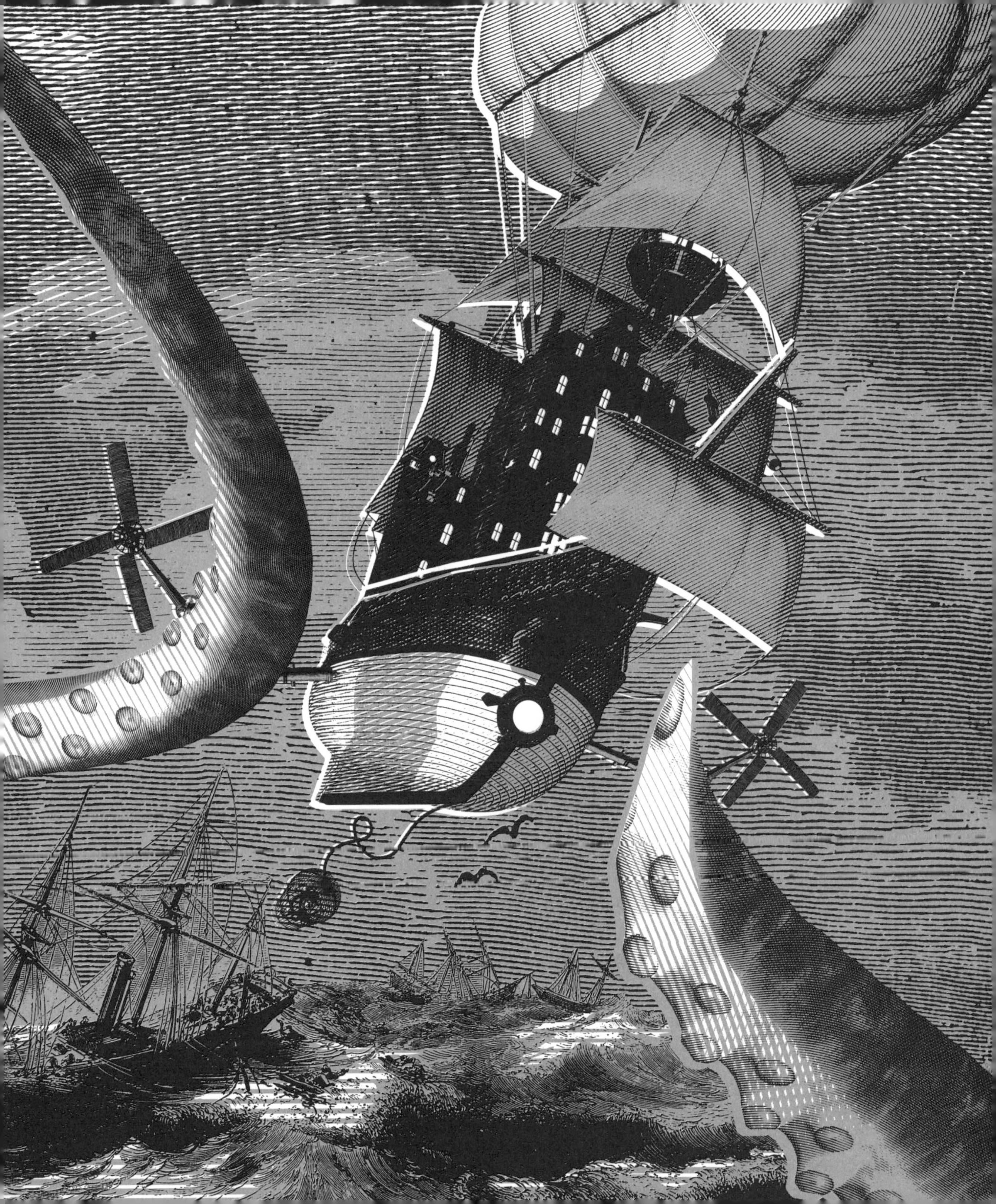

Warren couldn't believe his eyes. Eight enormous tentacles broke through the surface of the water, followed by an even more enormous bulbous head, blinking with seven eyes. The creature looked like Sketchy—only much, much larger. It was almost as large as the Warren Hotel!

"*BRRRRREEEEEEEEEEEEEE!*" it bellowed in a deep tone that rattled Warren's bones. Its eyes flashed angrily. It was furious!

The fighting froze as everyone stopped and stared. Even Jacques Rustyboots had forgotten about sawing at the rope. He gaped, agog, but then a broad smile stretched across his face and he began to laugh hysterically.

"The Great Eight!" he cried. "I've found it! At last!"

The Great Eight reached out a long tentacle toward the cage. Rustyboots spread out his arms as though looking for an embrace.

"Oh, Great Eight!" he said, his eyes shimmering. "I thought this day would never come!"

"*BRRRREEEEEEEEEEE!*" replied the Great Eight in its deafening baritone.

The tentacle curled around the cage, engulfing it. A second tentacle bent open the bars as if they were putty. Then a third reached for Sketchy, which crawled onto the enormous arm and embraced it with its own tentacles.

"Tweeeeeee!" Sketchy chirped happily.

"It's . . . your parent!" Warren said, realizing what was happening. "No wonder you're so happy!"

Still clinging to the cage, the Great Eight focused its eyes on Warren and Jacques Rustyboots, and a threatening rumble sounded deep in its belly. *"BRRRRRRRRRRRRRRR!"*

"O, Great Eight!" Rustyboots proclaimed loudly in his ringleader voice "I've searched for you for many long years, sailing in figure eights to prove my dedication and attract your attention. All my previous efforts were fruitless, but now I have earned your favor by bringing you what you seek—your beloved child! I await my glorious reward!"

The Great Eight's eyes narrowed.

"Uh-oh," Warren muttered.

With a sweep of its tentacle, the Great Eight tossed Warren and Jacques Rustyboots, cage and all, into its cavernous mouth.

"NOOOO!" Rustyboots cried.

Hot air, smelling of rotten fish, overwhelmed them as they slipped around on the Great Eight's slick tongue. The cage tumbled down its throat, plunging into darkness. Warren did not want to end up in its stomach, so he groped about for something to hang onto, managing to grab hold one of the creature's sharp teeth.

"This is all your fault!" Rustyboots snarled, waving his cutlass to and fro. "I should be getting rewarded right now, not eaten! This stupid creature thinks I'm with you! It thinks I'M the bad guy!"

Warren ducked, dodging Rustyboots's attack but losing his grip on the tooth and almost sliding down its throat. Somehow he managed to cling to the fleshy uvula dangling at the back of the Great Eight's mouth, using it to swing onto its giant tongue.

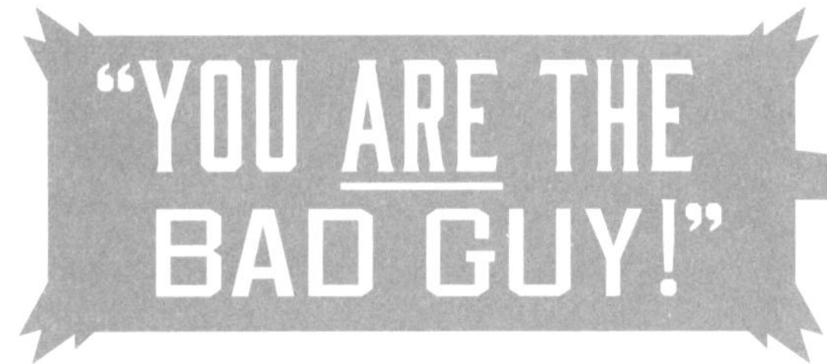

Warren cried. "You kidnapped Sketchy just so you could use it as bait!"

Rustyboots charged again and Warren dove once more, avoiding his blow.

"So what?" Rustyboots snapped. "What matters is that I've reunited the Great Eight with its child, so I should be given all the riches that it hoards under the sea! That's been my lifelong goal, and I won't let you stop me!"

Trying to regain his balance, Warren seized another tooth and found it to be wobbly. It popped out neatly in his hand. Now he had a weapon, too! He used it to block three more cutlass blows. But sharp as the tooth was, he wasn't willing to fight with

it—only defend.

"You can have the treasure for all I care!" Warren cried, parrying more strikes. "I just want my friend back!"

As they fought, Warren caught glimpses of the action taking place outside, and the picture wasn't pretty. The Great Eight was going ballistic! It was using its giant tentacles to wreak havoc, smashing ships and ripping apart the Sea Circus.

My friends! Warren thought, desperately. *They're still down there!*

In his distraction, he dodged a second too late. Rustyboots slashed at him again, managing to knock the tooth out of Warren's hands. It skittered to the back of the mouth and tumbled down the throat.

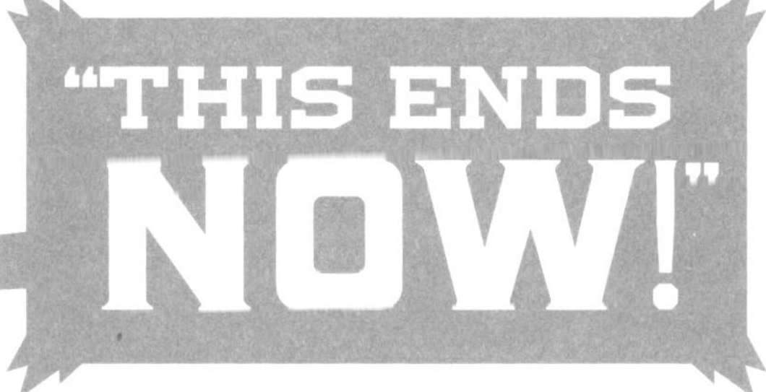

Rustyboots said, raising his cutlass for another blow.

Suddenly, a portal opened beside Warren, and Petula's head poked through. "I would have come sooner," she explained, "but I had to wait until I got a good glimpse of the inside of this thing's mouth!"

"Well, you're here now," Warren said, gratefully, and he leaped into the portal.

"Oh, no you don't!" Rustyboots cried, seizing Warren's leg. A game of tug-of-war ensued as Petula pulled Warren from one end and Rustyboots yanked on the other. Warren felt as though he might split in two—plus being half inside a portal didn't help.

Despite their combined efforts, Rustyboots proved stronger. With a loud grunt, he gave one final pull and both Warren and Petula fell out of the portal, bouncing back onto the fleshy tongue.

"Ha ha ha—AAAH!!" Rustyboots laughed, but then his boot slipped, and he lost his balance. He slid backward and, with an echoing cry, tumbled down the Great Eight's throat. Warren heard a distant splash as he landed in the creature's stomach.

Warren and Petula scrambled to avoid the same fate, slipping and sliding toward the shimmering portal.

But just as they were on the verge of reaching it, the Great Eight reared back and released an enormous *"ERRRRRRRRRRR-RRRRKKK!"*

The belch blasted Warren and Petula clear out of the Great Eight's mouth, along with a stream of hot, fetid air.

"AAAAH!" Warren cried as he and Petula soared through the air. Despite his terror, he couldn't help but notice the damage below. The ocean was littered with the demolished circus and pirate ships. Defeated pirates bobbed in the water, clinging to shards of wood.

"Hang on tight!" Petula cried, grabbing Warren's arm. "I'm going to try something crazy!"

"What?" Warren noticed that they were no longer flying but falling, faster and faster toward the water below. At this speed, they'd be flattened like pancakes upon hitting the surface.

"Drawing a portal in midair!" Petula gasped, and waved her arm.

Before Warren realized what was happening, Petula yanked him through and they landed with a hard *THUMP!* on the lobby floor. The Calm Waves pirates cheered at seeing Warren's face again.

"You did it, Petula!" Warren cried in relief. "Thanks for the save!"

"Anytime," Petula grumbled, shaking smelly strands of saliva off her hands.

"And thanks to all of you for defending the hotel," Warren told the crew. They, in turn, saluted him.

"Aye, aye, Captain!" Sharky said. "We held 'em off! Oh, how we missed being in a good ol' fashioned battle. Made us feel useful again!" The other pirates nodded in agreement.

"I'm so glad but... where are the others?" Warren asked. "Where are Chef Bunion and Uncle Rupert? Beatrice and Mr. Vanderbelly?"

"They're safe," Petula assured him. "They're down in the control room with Mr. Friggs and Captain Grayishwhitishbeard. Mom was able to get them out of the circus before the Great Eight smashed it to pieces."

"Oh, thank goodness!" Warren hurried to the lobby window and peered out. The Great Eight was still thrashing about, destroying every last remnant left in the sea. Only one tiny boat had managed to avoid being smashed; it was now disappearing into the distance as it made its escape. Warren could make out a tiny Sketchy, clinging to one of the Great Eight's tentacles. Was it scared? Or was it happy to be with its parent despite all the destruction?

"*BRRRRREEEEEEEEEE!*" the Great Eight bellowed. It slapped the water with its tentacles, sending debris flying.

"The Great Eight is still angry," Warren noticed, "but there's nothing left to destroy!"

Suddenly the creature paused, setting its

eyes upon the flying hotel.

"Spoke too soon!" Petula said.

The Great Eight began swimming toward the hotel at an alarming pace, reaching out with its long tentacles.

"We need to fly higher!" Warren cried, and he began running downstairs to the control room.

He burst through the door and saw Mr. Friggs at the controls, surrounded by the rest of his friends. But there was no time for pleasantries.

"Go up! Up!" he cried.

"I'm trying!" Friggs replied. "But those pesky circus pirates damaged several of our propellers. We can't fly as high as we used to."

There was a sickening *CRUNCH* and the hotel jerked as the Great Eight wrapped the entire structure in one of its enormous tentacles. Slimy suckers smothered the glass of the cockpit window.

"*BRRRRREEEEEEEEEE!*" it thundered, squeezing the building tighter and tighter.

Wood began to splinter and pop as the hotel was slowly crushed in its powerful grip.

"We're DOOOOOMED!" Rupert wailed.

Warren was at a loss for words. For once, he agreed with his uncle Rupert.

His beloved hotel, and everyone in it, was about to be obliterated.

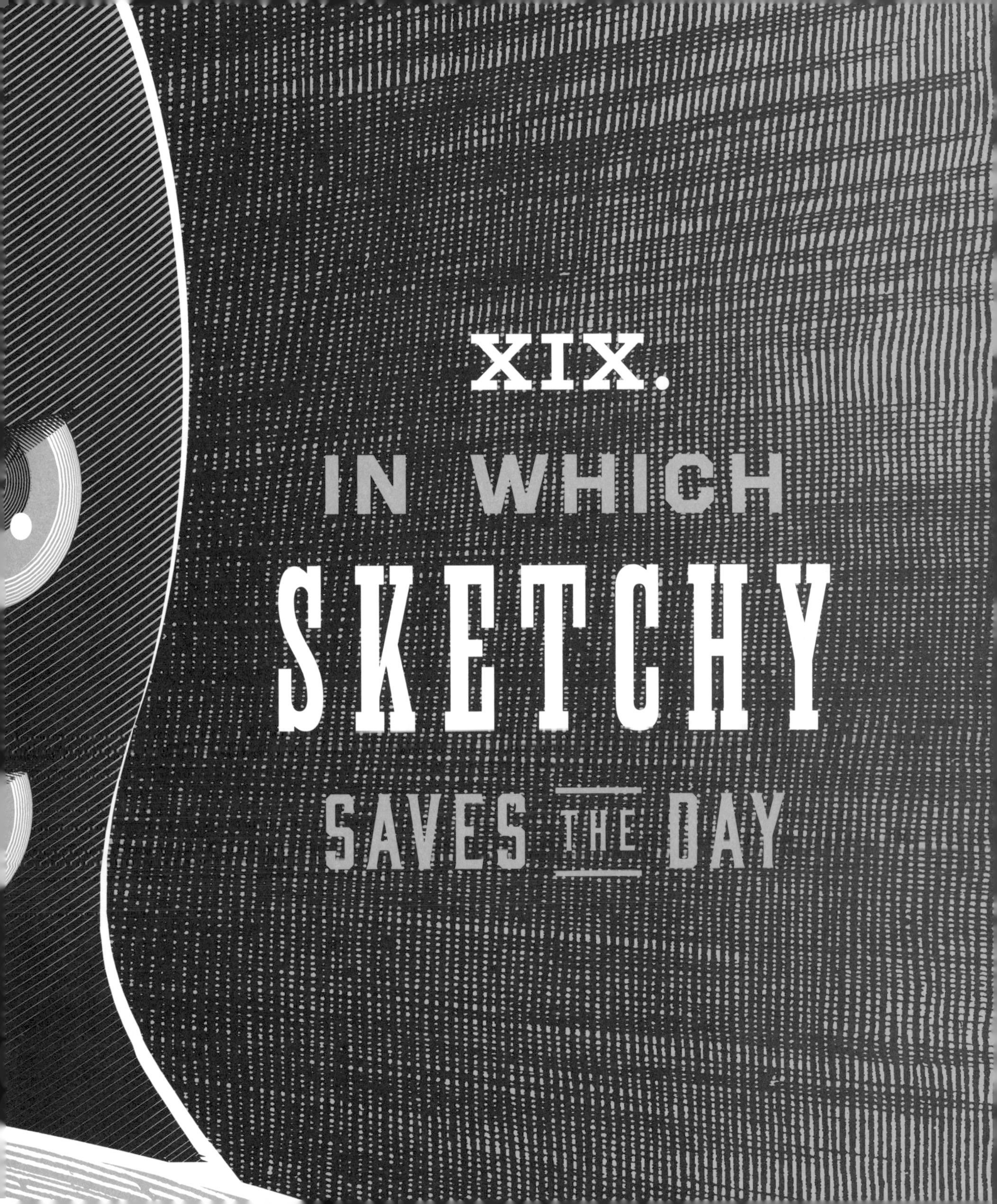

XIX.

IN WHICH SKETCHY SAVES THE DAY

Here was the ultimate proof that his curse was real, Warren decided. The hotel had survived for hundreds of years, through twelve generations, only to be destroyed on his own watch. The worst part was knowing there was nothing he could do. He couldn't stop a creature as big as the Great Eight, and he couldn't communicate with it, even if he wanted to. All he could do was watch everything he loved and worked so hard for be reduced to dust.

He exchanged sad looks with the rest of his friends . . . his family. They all shared his pain, and they huddled together in a group hug as they awaited the worst.

"All good things must come to an end," Mr. Friggs said softly.

"One day, someone will write a story about your legacy," Mr. Vandebelly added. "I'm just sorry it won't be me."

"Arr, you win some battles and ye lose some," Captain Grayishwhitishbeard noted. "That's the way of things."

"Your father would still be proud of you," Petula said, and Beatrice and Chef nodded in agreement.

"Well, I'm not proud of you," Uncle Rupert blubbered. "This is a disaster! Here I was, just enjoying my day at the circus, and now everything is ruined!"

Suddenly, a sharp whistle sounded: "TWEEEEEEEEEE!"

"Sketchy?" Warren said, breaking away from the group. He hurried to the window, but he could barely see past the Great Eight's tentacle. He ran back upstairs to the lobby and flung open the front door.

Sketchy was on the porch, holding out its tentacles protectively as it faced the Great Eight, who was looking at it in confusion.

"Sketchy!" Warren cried. "You came back!"

But his friend barely acknowledged him. It was focused entirely on the Great Eight.

"TWEEEEEE!" it shrilled.

"BRRREEEEEEEE?" the Great Eight rumbled back.

"Tweee! Tweeeeeee! Tweeeeeeeee!"

"BRRRRRRRRRREEEEEEEE."

Warren couldn't understand the whistles, but he knew what was happening. Sketchy was stopping its parent from destroying the hotel! It was telling the Great Eight that Warren and everyone aboard were its friends. Gently, the Great Eight released its grip, and everyone on board cheered in joy and relief.

"You did it, Sketchy! You saved us all!" Warren cried, hugging his beloved friend.

Sketchy wrapped its tentacles around Warren in a big hug. "Tweeeee!"

"FIRE!" shouted a familiar voice. Then a *BOOM!* and a flash of light.

"BRREEEEE?" The Great Eight whirled around in surprise as an enormous net fell over it, having been shot from a cannon aboard a tiny boat.

The boat Warren thought had been escaping had doubled back to attack! It was Bonny on board—with her parrot, too. She looked angrier than Warren had ever seen her.

"BREEEEEEE!" The Great Eight thrashed its tentacles, but only managed to entangle itself more within the netting. Warren winced—it looked painful the way the net dug into the Great Eight's rubbery skin.

"Release my grandpa this instant!" Bonny screamed, "or you're going to pay! I'll blast you out of the water if you don't cooperate!"

"BRRRRREEEEEEEEEE!" the Great Eight bellowed, and Sketchy whistled, too.

"We'll save it, Sketchy," Warren said to his friend. "We'll return the favor!"

He raced back down to the control room. The propellers might be slightly damaged, but the hotel could still fly. He could carry out his plan!

Warren steered the hotel toward the Great Eight, who was still thrashing about, growing more and more enraged by the second. On the boat, Bonny was busy prepping the cannon, stuffing it with sticks of dynamite.

Warren had to act fast—but he also had to be careful. With practiced skill, he edged the hotel as close to the Great Eight as he could and angled the propellers so they could cut through the rope.

"Warren!" Petula cried. "It's too risky! If you make a mistake, the propellers will hurt the Great Eight! Then it'll be even more angry!"

"Tweeeee?" Sketchy warbled anxiously.

"Trust me," Warren said, gritting his teeth. "I can do this!"

Just as he was within inches of the rope, a loud *BOOM!* exploded as the boat's cannon fired.

"BRRRRRRREEEEEEEE!!!!" The Great Eight ducked to the left, almost smashing into the hotel. Warren yanked on the controls, causing the flying ship to nosedive out of the way.

"Whhhhoooooaaa!" Petula cried while Sketchy trilled in fear.

Fireworks popped in the sky as the dynamite exploded in midair. *POP! POP! POP!*

Through the cockpit window, Warren could see Bonny stamping her feet angrily. Her tantrum was short-lived, however. She began stuffing more explosives into the cannon for another attempt.

The Great Eight was even more enraged, which made it difficult for Warren to pull in close. He had to bob and weave to avoid the flailing tentacles, not to mention the Great Eight's bulbous head as it swayed back and forth in frustration.

"Stand still!" Warren urged, even though he knew it couldn't hear him. Even if it could, he doubted it would listen.

Sketchy covered its eyes with its tentacles. "Tweeeeeeeee . . . "

Warren nudged the hotel close again, aiming just so . . .

SLICE!

. . . and then the propellers sliced through the netting, barely missing contact with the Great Eight's skin.

The net fell to pieces and disappeared into the waves. The Great Eight was free!

BOOM! Another blast of the cannon fired. Now free, the Great Eight was able to dodge it easily. It turned its flashing eyes toward the tiny boat and lunged at it. Bonny's jaw slackened in horror as she realized she could not stop such an enormous beast. It raised a gargantuan tentacle, preparing to bring it down and smash the boat to smithereens.

"NO!" Warren cried. He steered the hotel as fast as he could toward Bonny.

"Petula! Your portal!"

"You want me to save her?" Petula asked incredulously. "After everything she did to you?"

"Please!" Warren begged. "There's no time!"

Petula sighed and waved her hand.

She stepped through her portal just as the Great Eight's tentacle came smashing down on Bonny and her boat, obliterating it. Warren gasped. Was Petula too late?

Seconds later, he heard a *SHWOOP!* as a portal opened and Petula and Bonny tumbled onto the control room floor. McCrackers McCaw flew in behind them, seconds before the portal closed.

"RAWWWK!" he screeched, so stunned that he momentarily forget his words.

Bonny looked equally bewildered. "Why did you save me?"

"Because everyone deserves a second chance," Warren said. "Including your grandfather. I'm going to get him back, but violence isn't the answer." He turned to Sketchy. "Can you help me? I want to talk to the Great Eight."

Sketchy whistled and bobbed its head, and they went up to the lobby and opened the front door. The Great Eight was still thrashing about, smashing what was left of Bonny's boats into tiny fragments.

"TWEEEEEE!" Sketchy whistled sharply, catching its parent's attention.

The Great Eight blinked, seemingly coming out of its blind rage. Its head swiveled around and it reached a tentacle toward the front porch. Warren and Sketchy stepped onto the end.

"Twee, twee, twee!" Sketchy chirped.

"BRRRRREEE?" the Great Eight replied, slowly lifting Warren and Sketchy so they were level with its face.

"Great Eight," Warren said, "I'm sorry that you've had to deal with so many people mistreating you. But all this destruction won't do anything but continue the cycle of hate."

Sketchy translated for Warren, using a series of chirps, whistles, and tweets.

The Great Eight grumbled in response, narrowing its eyes. It didn't seem convinced.

"And I'm sorry that Sketchy was stolen from you years ago. That must have been really hard. But now you've separated Bonny from her grandfather, and that's not right, either. I know they're not perfect, and they've made some mistakes, but they're family, and family should be together."

Sketchy translated again, and the Great Eight sighed heavily as it absorbed Warren's words.

Slowly, it opened its enormous mouth and reached a tentacle down its throat. Seconds later, it pulled out a very soggy and very smelly Jacques Rustyboots.

"Gramps!" Bonny cried.

The Great Eight dumped the pirate unceremoniously onto the deck and grumbled noisily.

Bonny and her grandfather embraced. "Gramps, I was so scared."

"Me, too, Bonny," Rustyboots said. "All that time down there got me thinking... maybe it's time to retire. There's no treasure

in the world worth sitting in a pile of fish guts for. Or being separated from my only granddaughter."

"You mean, you're coming back to Calm Waves?" Bonny asked hopefully. "WE'RE GOING HOME?"

"That's right," Rustyboots said, smiling. "Once and for all."

The elderly pirates cheered from the lobby. Warren was sad to think of his childhood idol abandoning adventure and settling down into a quiet life of retirement, but given what Jacques Rustyboots had been up to lately, he knew it was for the best. Besides, he'd always have the books to read and enjoy.

"Thank you, Sketchy," Warren said. "And thank you, Great Eight. We'll leave you in peace now."

He took one of Sketchy's arms. "Come on, Sketchy. Let's go home."

But Sketchy pulled its tentacle away. "Tweeeee . . ."

"What's wrong?" Warren asked, looking at his friend in confusion.

Sketchy shook its bulbous head. "Tweeee."

Warren may not have spoken Sketchy's language, but it was all too clear what it was trying to say. "You—you mean, you want to stay here? With the Great Eight?"

Sketchy chirped sadly, but nodded its head.

"Of course," Warren said, finally understanding. "This is your parent, after all. This is your true home." He felt as though his heart were breaking into a million pieces, but he couldn't let Sketchy know how much it hurt.

Petula appeared beside them, having popped through a portal, and she flung her arms around Sketchy.

"Oh, I'm going to miss you so much!"

Sketchy hugged her tight and whistled sadly.

Warren blinked back tears. "Well, I guess this is goodbye."

Suddenly, Sketchy grabbed Petula's and Warren's hands with its tentacles and began chirping loudly. "Twee! Twee! Twee!"

"You want us to come with you?" Warren asked. "I'm sorry Sketchy. We can't live underwater."

But it continued to tug on their hands.

"Warren," Petula said, "I think it wants to show us something."

XX.

IN WHICH SKETCHY RETURNS HOME

ketchy chirped something at the Great Eight, and it nodded its giant head in response. Then Sketchy jumped off its parent's tentacle and splashed into the water below. The Great Eight followed, wrapping Warren and Petula securely in its tentacle as it submerged itself under the sea.

"No, no!" Warren cried. "We can't breathe underwater! Stop!"

"Hold your breath!" Petula shouted seconds before they splashed beneath the surface.

Warren did so, puffing out his cheeks as cold water engulfed him. The Great Eight released its grip and they clung together, kicking their legs.

"BRRRRREEEEEEEEEEE," the Great Eight bellowed, its voice amplified underwater. An enormous bubble emerged from its mouth and surrounded Warren and Petula, encasing them in air.

"Good, because I was almost out of air!" Warren gasped.

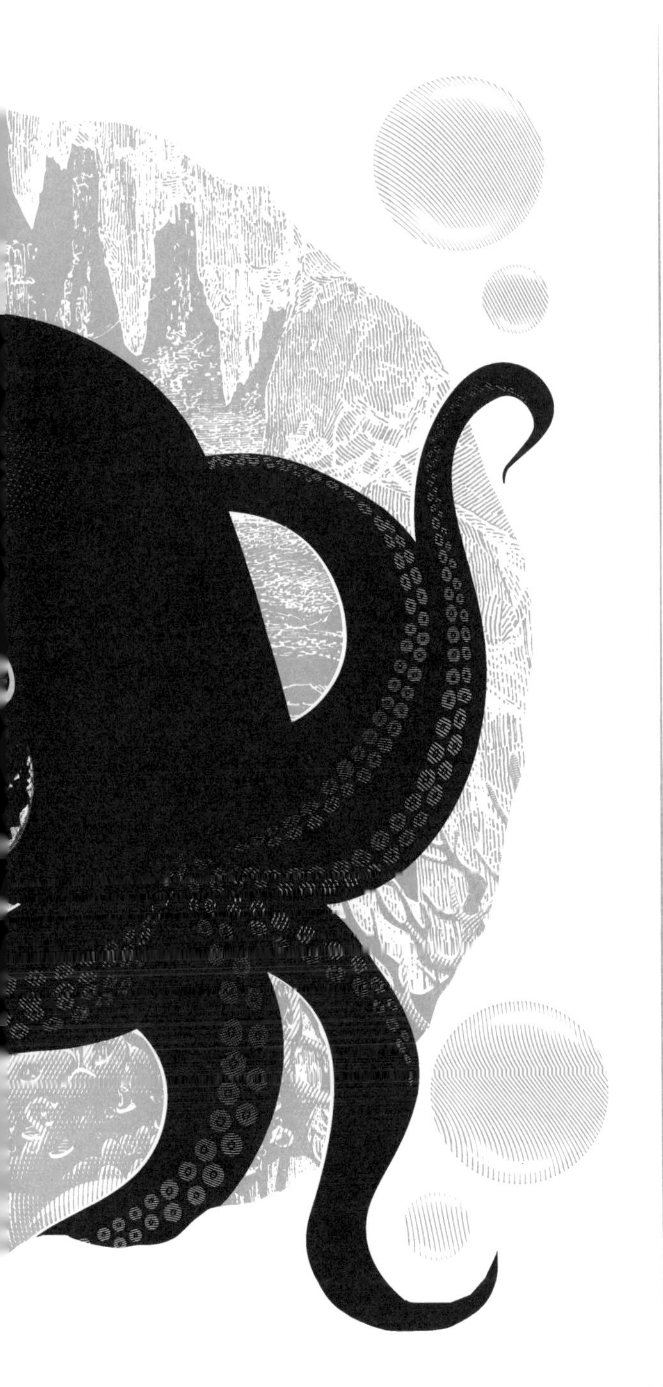

"Tweeeee!" Sketchy warbled from nearby, and beckoned them with its tentacle. The Great Eight followed, moving far more gracefully underwater than it did above the surface. Warren and Petula followed, too, encased in their protective bubble. Deeper and deeper they went as they followed Sketchy and the Great Eight toward the mouth of a glistening underwater cavern. Their home.

Inside, the enormous cave sparkled with minerals and phosphorescent coral. There was no gold. No treasure. The legend of the Great Eight's horde was just a fairy tale, Warren realized.

But the walls were completely covered in drawings, elegant pictographs drawn with bioluminescent charcoal.

"Looks like Sketchy's parent is a bit of an artiste, too!" Warren said, taking it all in.

"Twee! Twee!" Sketchy chirped, pointing to one wall.

"Warren, I think the pictures tell a story," Petula said.

Warren scanned the drawings, but as lovely as they were, he had trouble deciphering them.

"Don't worry," Petula assured him. "Thanks to my mom, I'm fluent in pictographs. Here, I'll translate for you . . ."

Long ago, Sketchy lived happily with its parent and siblings under the sea . . .

Sketchy was the most playful of all the siblings. One day it got distracted while chasing a little clam and strayed too far from home.

It realized it was lost and tried to find its way back, but it only traveled farther and farther away from home . . .

After a few days, it noticed a boat and swam toward it, hoping it might be able to help.

That boat was Jacques Rustyboots's pirate ship, and it was searching for the Great Eight. He ended up catching Sketchy instead.

Meanwhile, the Great Eight realized Sketchy was missing and searched for it far and wide. It caused terrible storms everywhere it went.

Eventually, it ran into the little clam, who told it what had happened to Sketchy.

The Great Eight knew it would never see Sketchy again. It retreated to its cave in sorrow and could not be consoled.

"BRRRRRREEEE," the Great Eight rumbled, wrapping a tentacle around Sketchy.

"That's so sad," Warren said. "Even after my grandfather rescued you from Jacques Rustyboots, you still weren't where you belonged. You must have been so scared."

Sketchy chirped and nodded sadly. It picked up a piece of glowing chalk and began scribbling furiously on the walls, drawing its own pictographs. Warren turned, trying to decipher them.

"Petula?" he asked.

"One second," she said. "I think I understand . . ."

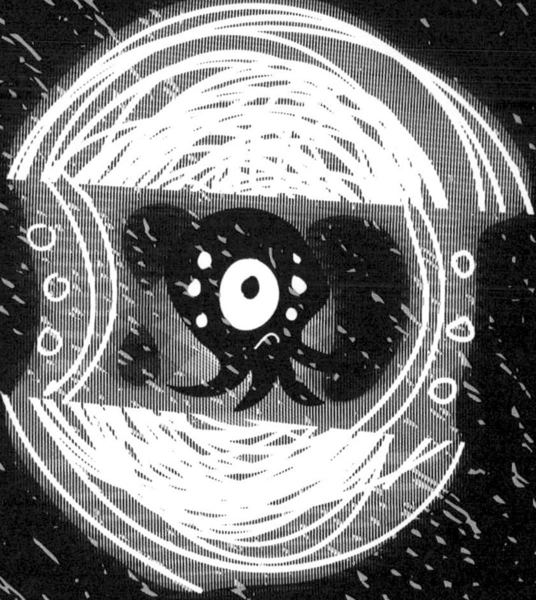

At first it hid in the
pipes of the hotel,
until it grew too large
to fit comfortably.

Eventually it made its way to the
boiler room. The rumbling sounds
the boiler made reminded it of the
Great Eight, so Sketchy felt safe
there. It reminded it of home.

It stayed hidden there for many years,
learning the secrets of the hotel.
Over time, it took pride in its new
home and guarded its secrets well.

It wasn't until you showed up, Warren, that Sketchy
felt like it had a family again. That's why it decided
to help you find the All-Seeing Eye after avoiding
your father and grandfather for so many years.

Petula finished telling the story, and Warren nodded, tears in his eyes. "I'm glad I found you, too, Sketchy. You're the first friend I ever had. I'll always be grateful for that."

"Tweeee!" Sketchy trilled happily.

"Twee! Twee! Twee!" A chorus of whistles surrounded them as dozens of little Sketchies came out of hiding. They emerged from behind rocks and plants and little hidey-holes in the sand. They circled around Sketchy, chirping happily.

"Your siblings!" Warren said, grinning. "They're welcoming you home!"

"BRRREEEEEEEEEE!" rumbled the Great Eight, encircling all of its children, along with Warren and Petula, in a loving embrace.

Warren put his hand against the surface of the bubble. "I'm going to miss you," he said to Sketchy. "But I'm happy you're home. This is where you belong."

Sketchy let out a sad warble as it wrapped its tentacles around Warren and Petula's bubble.

"It's time for us to go," Warren said, choking back tears. "Take care of yourself, Sketchy."

Warren and Petula sniffled as they floated upward. Sketchy and all its siblings waved their tentacles goodbye, chirping like a tree full of birds. The Great Eight added its musical baritone to the mix.

They eventually broke the surface of the water and saw the hotel bobbing nearby. Warren could see the smiling faces of Mr. Friggs, Chef Bunion, Beatrice, Mr. Vanderbelly, and even Uncle Rupert from where they stood on the porch. They all held out their arms, pulling Petula and Warren onboard.

"We were startin' to get worried!" Chef cried, encompassing Warren in a big bear hug. "We thought you might want to stay down there forever!"

"And leave my family?" Warren said, smiling back. "No way!"

It wasn't until they had set a course for the retirement island and sailed away that Warren realized he had completely forgotten to ask the Great Eight to remove his family's curse.

Well, he reasoned, just as the Great Eight didn't really guard a horde of treasure, it wasn't likely to have magical curse-breaking abilities either.

Some legends were just that—stories to ignite the imagination and inspire action.

Epilogue

Thanks for showing us that we still have some adventure left in our old bones!" Sharky said to Warren.

"Aye, aye!" cheered the rest of the elderly pirates.

The hotel was anchored just outside the Calm Waves Retirement Home for the Formerly Sea-Faring and Adventurous, and Warren was helping his guests check out. He shook each wrinkled hand as the pirates departed.

"I couldn't have saved Sketchy without your help," Warren said. "You all worked so hard, and now you deserve a break."

CLANG! CLANG! CLANG! Jacques Rustyboots was banging a pot with a spoon from where he stood on the beach. He wore a frilly apron, and flour dusted his nose.

"Chow time!" he announced. "It's pancakes for dinner!"

"I'm gonna mish all that fanshy hotel food," the toothless pirate grumbled as he shambled off with the others.

"Quit complainin'!" Bonny said.

"Looks like Rustyboots is adjusting rather quickly to being retired," Petula noted.

"Arrgh, give him time," Captain Grayishwhitishbeard grumbled. "He'll get bored and be off on some other venture before you know it."

"As long as it doesn't involve kidnapping," Warren said.

"So, is this farewell, Captain?" Petula said. "You don't want your pancakes to get cold."

"Arrgh, if it's all the same to you, I'd much rather join yer crew. Rustyboots and I don't get along, and I'm too hale and hearty to be retired!"

"Of course!" Warren said gratefully. "I'd love to have another hand at the controls."

Captain Grayishwhitishbeard saluted them and turned to go inside. "Yarr, I'll fire her up and get 'er ready to go!"

"Ahem," Bonny said, approaching Warren. She scowled and kicked the sand. "I just wanted to say, um, thanks. And sorry for all the trouble I caused. I just wanted to impress my gramps and help him find the Great Eight. It's all I've ever heard him talk about. But I was unfair to you, even though you were so nice to me."

Warren understood. "It's O.K. I know I'd feel the same way if I was related to the famous Jacques Rustyboots. By the way—do you think he would sign my novels before we go?"

"I already took care of it," Bonny said with a wink. "Check your bookcase later!"

"Thanks, Bonny!"

"Well, I guess this is goodbye," she replied, blushing. Before Warren could respond, she turned and ran toward the Calm Waves building. Seconds later, she turned around and yelled, "And good luck with your curse!"

"Oh, really!" Petula sighed. "Some things never change."

"Well, even if I was cursed, I think it's broken now," Warren said. "And I didn't even need the Great Eight to do it for me."

"How's that?"

"Well, I was thinking . . . if it's a thirteen-year curse, that could mean the curse lasts for thirteen years, rather than being a curse that starts when you're thirteen years old," he explained. "I've had an unlucky life so far, but now that I'm thirteen, things are looking up. I've got friends and family that I love, and a hotel that can walk, swim, and fly. It doesn't get much better than that!"

"That's true," Petula said. "So where should we go next?"

"Let's find out!" Warren said.

And he and Petula raced back into the Warren Hotel, laughing all the way.

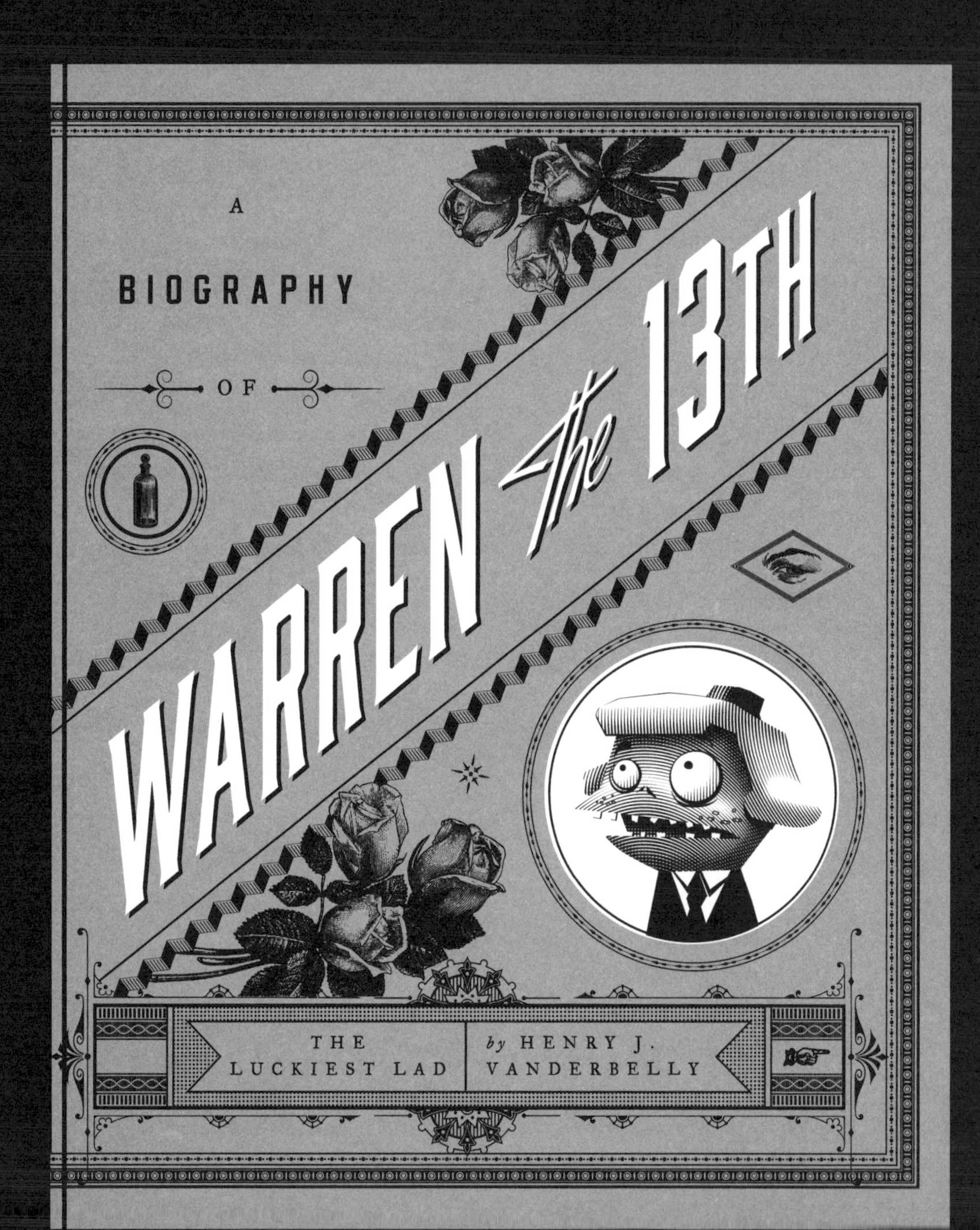
A
BIOGRAPHY
OF
WARREN the 13TH
THE
LUCKIEST LAD
by HENRY J.
VANDERBELLY

n any given day, look up. You might see a strange shape in the sky, blotted against the sun. Do not be alarmed, for it is just the Marvelous World-Famous Warren Hotel making its rounds across the globe. See it soar through the clouds like a bird and watch it swoop over the pointed treetops of the Malwoods, emerging over the resort known as the Sap Caldera, where sapsquatches frolic and play.

On other days you might spot it marching across Fauntleroy, pausing at the crater that used to be its home. Remnants of an old hedge maze still remain there, as well as a statue of Warren the 1st—the originator of this mighty hotel—gone but never forgotten.

And on yet another day, you might spot the hotel sailing across the seas, flying its flag proudly as its inhabitants wave merrily to dozens of tentacled creatures who have gathered round to say hello [*chief among them a special little creature by the name of Sketchy, who whistles a happy tune when greeting its dear friend, Warren the* 13*th*].

True, this odd hotel may carry an equally strange crew consisting of a circus chef, a former adventurer turned historian, a perfumier, and an importer-exporter, among others. But when you stay at the hotel as a guest, be assured that you will be warmly welcomed and treated with world-class hospitality.

For as the young Warren the 13th likes to say, when you stay at the Warren, you're family.

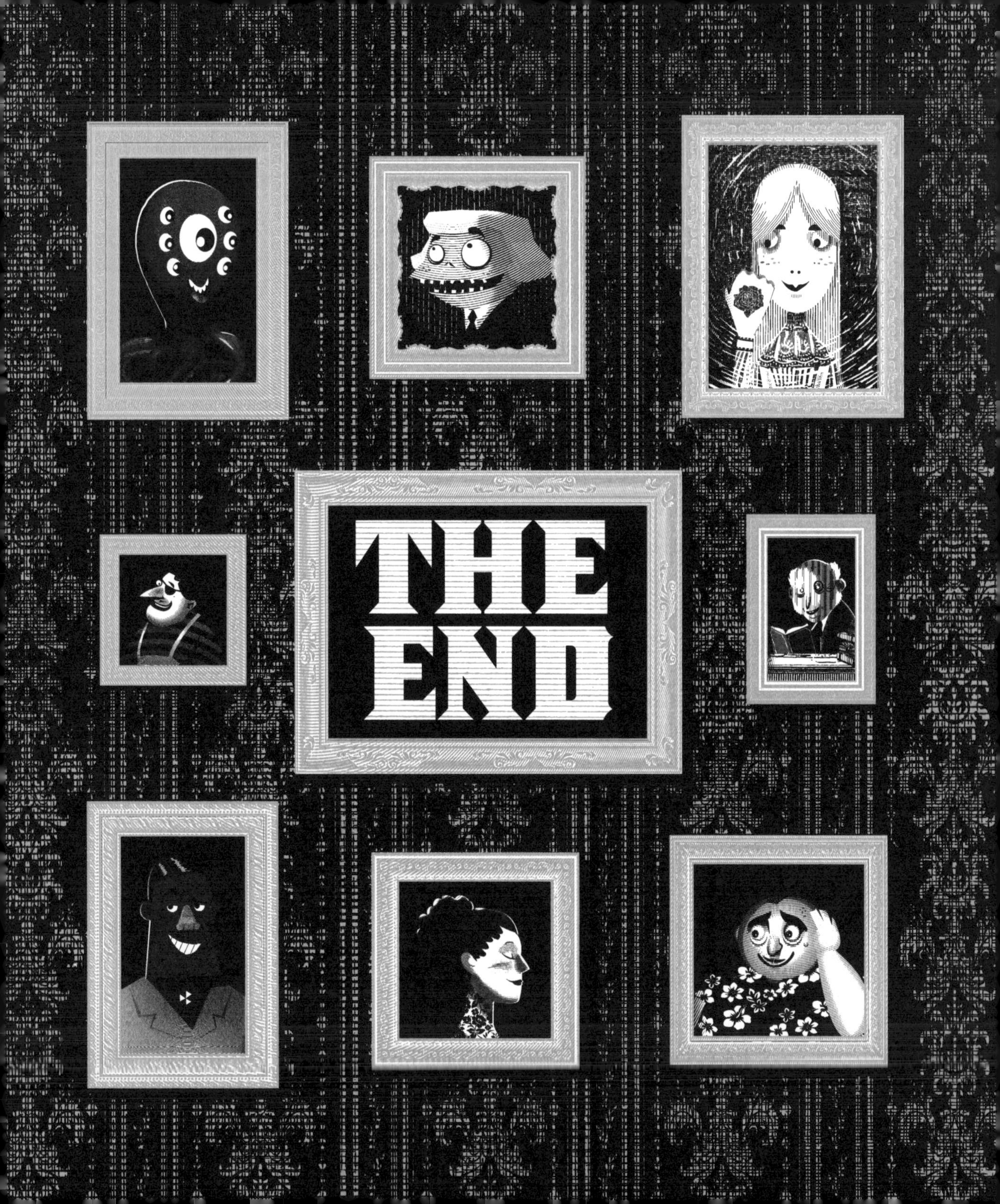
THE END

Acknowledgments

Thank you to everyone who has been on this amazing ride with the entire "Warren family" for these past three volumes.

Somehow, I magically forget each and every time how much work every volume of Warren is. The art alone takes months and months to complete, and there are times where I find my eyes crossing from staring at black and white lines, and it's difficult to push through. It's during these times [often weekends] that I remind myself how lucky I am to tell Warren's story. And when that doesn't work . . . I think about the tens of thousands of students that we have spoken to at various schools over the years, and the wonderful drawings and cards that they've sent us. A big thank-you to all the fans who have kept us going.

First off, thanks to everyone at Quirk Books. I can't imagine Warren living elsewhere. As always, a special thanks to Jason Rekulak, who brought Warren into Quirk initially and believed in us from the very start.

On a personal note, thank you to my partner, Hanh. You have been entirely supportive of the Warren books and my various creative endeavors. You are truly amazing.

Thanks to my small, but wonderful family; Mom, Dad, Ira, and Eli. And to all of the Staehles, Baxters, Loan, and the rest of Hanh's family for their years of supporting Warren.

Thanks to Atom, Rich, Roberto, Fearn, Steve, Rob, Jacob, Rex, Philip, Alex, Evan, Matteo, Jake, Aaron, Eric, Christine, Mike, Raina, Trevor, Susan, Lauren, Corey, Doogie, Laura, Cricket, James, Amber, Kazu, Jim, Ed, and Fred & Jeanne for all of their support.

Thanks to all of my friends and supporters over the years from Harper, and JibJab, and Epic.

Last but certainly not least, a huge hotel-sized thanks to Tania del Rio for undertaking this project with me, and for dedicating so much of her time and effort to it.

It's been such a challenging but fun job to work on this trilogy, and to spend so much time with Warren, Petula, Sketchy, Beatrice, Friggs, Chef Bunion, Mr. Vanderbelly, Uncle Rupert, and the rest of the crew. We hope you enjoy the books as as much as we enjoyed making them.

Until next time!

-Will.

Acknowledgments

First and foremost, I'd like to thank Will Staehle for bringing me along on this fantastic journey – I hope we'll have a chance to collaborate again in the future! Thanks to our original editor Jason Rekulak, who was so influential to the series. I hope we've done you proud. I'm grateful to Rebecca Gyllenhaal for taking over the reins, as well as Brett Cohen, Jhanteigh Kupihea, Nicole De Jackmo, Katherine McGuire, Rick Chillot, Kelsey Hoffman, Christina Schillaci, Megan DiPasquale, Mary Ellen Wilson, Ivy Noelle Weir, and the rest of the awesome Quirk team. I'm thankful for the team at Gotham for all you've done for Warren behind the scenes. I'm so grateful to Paul Crichton for organizing an awesome school tour, and for all the teachers, librarians, and students who welcomed us and made us feel like superstars! To all the fans who have emailed me or sent me letters, thank you so much!

To my fellow authors and writers who have welcomed me into the fold and have shown me special kindness, a very special thanks to Paul Krueger, Jane Espenson, Gene Ha, Sherri L. Smith, Brad T. Gottfred, Livia Blackburne, Ashley Poston, C.B Lee, and Maritere Bellas.

Thank you Maria Stout, Uriel Walker, and John "Dandan" Phillips for your cheerleading, and for being awesome friends, both online and off.

Liz and Terry Adams, Krishna Devine, Zach Baker, and Chris Straeter, I truly appreciate your friendship and support. Huge thanks to my coworkers and dear friends Brian Randolph, Ashley Thayer, and Ray Anthony Barrett III for letting me vent about writing, publishing, and everything in-between. Thank you to Mark Grotjahn and Ana Vejzovic Sharp for your support and giving me the time to go on my book tour.

I have so much gratitude for my family. To my mom and dad, Rita and Israel del Rio, thank for your love, optimism, and support. Thanks to my brothers Derek and Alex del Rio [especially for the help with that pesky puzzle!] Thanks to my aunts Jerry, Sylvia, and Louise Sabo for your support and for spreading the word about the Warren books!
I'm grateful to my in-laws; Lakshmi, Jerry, and Will Hackett, and Prudence and Greg Daniels – I'm so lucky to have you in my corner!

And, last but not least, thank you to my husband, Sebastian Hackett, who has been my number one fan and a voice of reason and encouragement when I'm suffering from writers' block or imposter syndrome. I hope I can support your dreams as much as you've supported mine.

Goddess, I'm grateful for the gift of this experience. Thank you, thank you, thank you!

–Tania

WILL STAEHLE

is the creator of Warren the 13th, and is an award-winning designer and illustrator. He grew up reading comics and working summers at his parent's design firm in Wisconsin. He now spends his days designing book covers, posters, and mini-comics, to ensure that he gets as little sleep as possible. He lives in Seattle.

unusualco.com

 *@unusualcorp*

TANIA DEL RIO

is a professional comic book writer and artist who has spent the past 15 years writing and illustrating, primarily for a young audience. Her clients include Archie Comics, Dark Horse, and Marvel; she is best known for her work writing and drawing a 42-issue run of *Sabrina the Teenage Witch*. She lives in Los Angeles.

taniadelrio.com

@taniadelrio